'Please say you me. No interru and me togethe night ahead of u

Charlotte held her breath. The whole idea was so fabulously exciting. A whole night in Iannis's arms… But it didn't make sense any more. Not after what she'd just heard. A relationship with Iannis could turn out just as disastrous as the one she'd experienced with James. Iannis was theoretically divorced, theoretically free, but all the complications would always be there in the background.

She stared up at him, her treacherous body trying to tempt her into a night of passion while her conscious, sensible mind was saying she should run from here and stay away.

'So what's it to be, Charlotte?'

Margaret Barker has enjoyed a variety of interesting careers. A State Registered Nurse and qualified teacher, she holds a degree in French and Linguistics and is a Licentiate of the Royal Academy of Music. As a full-time writer, Margaret says, 'Writing is my most interesting career because it fits perfectly into my happy life as a wife, mother and grandmother. My husband and I live in an idyllic sixteenth-century house near the East Anglian coast. Our grown-up children have flown the nest, but they often fly back again, bringing their own young families with them for wonderful weekend and holiday reunions.'

Recent titles by the same author:

THE FRENCH SURGEON'S SECRET CHILD
DR SOTIRIS'S WOMAN
DR DEMTRIUS'S DILEMMA
DR MICHAELIS'S SECRET

THE GREEK DOCTOR'S BRIDE

BY

MARGARET BARKER

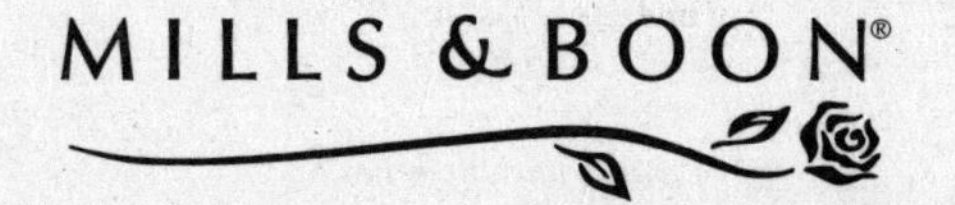

First published in Great Britain 2004
Harlequin Mills & Boon Limited,
Eton House, 18-24 Paradise Road, Richmond, Surrey TW9 1SR

ISBN 0 263 83887 0

Set in Times Roman 10½ on 12 pt.
03-0304-50273

Printed and bound in Spain
by Litografia Rosés, S.A., Barcelona

CHAPTER ONE

'DON'T worry about your luggage,' the young Greek had said as he'd thrown Charlotte's belongings onto an open truck.

He'd offered Charlotte a lift in the tiny cab of the antiquated three-wheeled vehicle parked precariously on the edge of the busy harbour, but she'd said she preferred to walk. She'd badly needed some fresh air after being cooped up for hours without stretching her legs, first on the plane and then on the ferry from Athens.

The young Greek had given her a strange look, as if unable to understand why anyone would prefer to walk when they could ride, before telling Charlotte to follow the only road over the hill for about ten minutes. She couldn't miss it, apparently.

Charlotte wasn't in the least bit worried about her luggage. As she trekked along the ancient cobbled track from the harbourside over the brow of the hill she reflected that that was the least of her worries. Anyway, she'd packed nothing of value for this six-month assignment working in a Greek island clinic. The thing that worried her most was meeting up with the medical director of the clinic. At her interview in London she'd had the distinct impression that her new boss might be something of a difficult person to work for.

She'd been asked if she was absolutely sure that she would be able to cope with life on a small Greek island where she knew nobody. She would find that the working conditions were very different from working in a large

London hospital with high-tech equipment and continual support from her colleagues. Apparently the medical director of the clinic on Lirakis had asked the agency to make sure that the candidate they chose would be able to cope with medical emergencies as they arose on the island and would be strong enough to complete the full six months of the assignment.

Charlotte paused to glance back at the rough, bumpy road she'd walked up from the harbour. A thin layer of concrete had been spread over the uneven stones but part of this had buckled in the heat. A couple of roadmen were beginning work on the difficult section, swinging their pick-axes to remove the surface they'd recently made. The sweat was already glistening on their bare brown arms. The mid-morning heat was building up. And it was only May! What would it be like as the summer progressed?

Wow, the view was fantastic! Charlotte balanced herself on a boulder at the side of the road as she paused to take in the full panorama. Down there by the harbour, the weather-beaten old ferry she'd arrived on was pulling out to go to another island. Tiny fishing boats returning with the morning's catch had moved out of its way like kittens avoiding a marauding tiger. The sun was shining on the clear, turquoise, opalescent water and warming the houses clustered around the bay.

She could see a beautiful church with a bell tower almost on the edge of the water. It looked as if one huge wave would carry it away into the harbour and yet, over the years, it had somehow managed to survive the onslaught of the seasons. There must have been good craftsmen on the island in the days when the church was built. It certainly looked as if the inhabitants took a great pride in their church and made sure it was kept in good repair. No peeling paint or leaking roofs here.

Reluctantly, Charlotte tore herself away from admiring the view and turned back to follow the track over the hill. The scenery on the other side was equally spectacular. She could see a wide bay with a tiny village of white-walled, red-roofed cottages nestling by the water, watched over by rugged hills. The cluster of white buildings in the trees at the end of the village looked as if it housed the clinic where she was going to work. Apart from a taverna where wooden chairs and tables had been arranged outside under a striped awning, there was no other sign of habitation.

She could just make out a couple of swimmers in the water at the far end of the bay. Raising her eyes to the hills, Charlotte saw the outline of a ruined Crusader castle perched on the edge of a cliff. The sheer drop down to the sea below looked as if it would have been a deterrent to any intruders who'd tried to scale it. The castle must have been completely impregnable. What stories of long ago the islanders would be able to recount! As well as learning the language, she found herself longing to find out more about the island's history and the people who'd lived here.

She took a deep breath. Once she'd met the doctor she was going to work with she would be able to appreciate the beauty of this island more fully. But, for the moment, the butterflies in her stomach were doing a war dance. And the uncomfortable seat on the late-night flight, exacerbated by the seemingly endless waiting around in both airports, had meant she'd lost a whole night's sleep.

Her London flat seemed suddenly so far away and so appealingly comfortable! Yesterday, she'd been glad to leave it, to get away from the memories for a while, but now, weary from lack of sleep, she was beginning to question what she was doing here. Why couldn't she have stayed and simply put the phone down on James every time he'd tried to reach her? She'd changed the locks and her mobile number, so why hadn't she had the number in the apartment changed and gone ex-directory? Had she still been clinging to the past, unable to let go?

She paused for a moment to catch her breath.The smell of herbs from the hills was beautiful. For a few moments she tried to lose herself in the peace and tranquillity of the landscape.

Yes, this was the right course of action! Six months in which to forget James and plan what she wanted to do next. Once she'd met her new boss and found out what he was really like, she would feel better. He couldn't be as difficult as she'd imagined, could he? The interviewer in London said he'd never met Dr Iannis Kimolakis but he'd heard that he could be a very exacting man to work for.

Quite frankly, Charlotte had been surprised to get the job. She was confident that she was a good doctor with an excellent track record, but it wasn't as if she even spoke Greek, although she'd bought a teach-yourself-Greek book and had got stuck into learning it since she'd been appointed. There'd been several other candidates waiting outside when she'd left the interview. She'd wondered if any of them, like her, were anxious to leave their troubles behind and go out to an idyllic Greek island. Were any of them seeking an answer to the daunting question, What shall I do now that I'm trying to change the direction of my life and feel as if I'm floundering around and getting nowhere?

The island might be idyllic, but what about the working conditions? she wondered as she walked through the clinic gates. The front section of the clinic was obviously original, neoclassical in style. The ornate, very beautiful stonework looked as if it had survived a few violent storms and been patched up here and there. A survivor, like she was. She felt an immediate bond with the place.

The surrounding buildings were later additions, but built in an appealingly style that blended well with the surroundings. She decided she'd better check in and find out where she was going to live for the next six months. When she'd received the letter telling her that her application had been successful she'd also been informed that accommodation would be provided by the clinic.

She slowed her step. A tall man was coming out of the main door. He paused and waited. This couldn't be Dr Iannis Kimolakis, could it? He wouldn't come out in person to meet her. No, this would be one of his minions. But a very nice minion! Tall, dark, handsome in a classic sort of way, nevertheless he had a rugged frame and was built like a rugby player.

Did they play rugby in Greece? She suppressed a nervous giggle. This man would be difficult to tackle. Smart chinos, open-necked shirt, dark chest hair protruding above the second button. Very casual but a bit stern-looking.

She told herself to walk a bit quicker and look purposeful! Didn't want to give this messenger the impression she was nervous. He was sure to report back to the boss that—

'Dr Charlotte Manners?'

The good-looking Greek was holding out his hand towards her, but he wasn't smiling. Well, why should he? She probable looked a complete wreck in her crumpled denim jacket and trousers, dusty suede boots and shiny, make-up-less face. Her face felt decidedly damp with sweat. She'd once read somewhere that horses sweated, men perspired and ladies glowed. If that was so then she must have a face that glowed like a beacon! She wished she'd made the effort to check her appearance and slap on some lipstick.

Charlotte's hand was grasped in a very strong grip. She stifled the gasp of something akin to pain, at the same time ignoring the spark of a kind of electric current as it shot up her arm. Even though the man looked terrifyingly unapproachable and solemn, she found herself fascinated by his eyes. Dark, soulful, deep pools you could drown in if you felt like losing all your inhibitions and—

'I'm Iannis Kimolakis. You must be Dr Charlotte Manners.'

The voice was deep, gravelly, sexy almost if you could overcome your fear of the power that seemed to exude from his every pore. This huge hand grasping hers felt as if it could fell a tree with one blow. She removed her hand quickly, as if she'd been burnt. Her green eyes widened as she stared up at Dr Kimolakis. He was tall, very tall. She was by no means short but her neck would certainly find it a strain to keep up a standing conversation with this man.

'You're not what I… How do you do? I mean…' She hesitated. Go for it, girl! Try out that Greek phrase in chapter one. *'Ti kanis?'*

Not a flicker of a smile at her feeble attempt.

'I think you mean *ti kanete*, Dr Manners.' The cool reply was in impeccable English, with a slight, but decidedly charming hint of a Greek accent. 'If you've only just met someone it's better to use the more formal expression when you're asking the person how he is.'

He paused as if to emphasise the point. 'If you'd like to come inside we can have a short discussion about your duties.'

Weren't the Greeks supposed to be a warm, hospitable people? Especially the islanders? Following her boss, Charlotte reflected that when she'd spent a couple of weeks on Corfu as a child she'd found the Greeks delightful. Dr Kimolakis was everything she'd feared he might be except he was packaged in a different way to her expectations. She'd expected a mature, older man, set in his ways. Iannis

Kimolakis was housed in a disarmingly boyish, indisputably handsome body. The sort of body that years ago, long before James, would have set her pulses racing.

He was opening the door to a room with his name on it.

'Do come in, Dr Manners.'

'Thank you, Dr Kimolakis.'

Charlotte followed meekly, wondering whether to close the door or not. Oh, let him close his own door! This was ludicrous! The stern voice, the forbidding expression on his face. How could she work with a man like this? Maybe, because of his superb physique, he thought he was God's gift to women. If so, why didn't he turn on the charm? Get her to eat out of his hand? Which she wasn't going to do any more. Not now that she'd sworn never to give in to another man for the rest of her life.

Well, perhaps not life. Life is a long time and she didn't know how she would feel in ten years' time. Let's just say for the foreseeable future. Or at least until some of the James-inflicted emotional wounds have healed. Charlotte sat down on the brown leather chair in front of the surly doctor's desk. She'd practised a winning smile as she'd walked down the corridor. Now was the time to try it out. See if she could melt his ice-cold exterior, get through that outer layer of…

No, he hadn't even noticed. He was reading something on the desk. Her CV and the report about her interview it looked like from this side of the desk, although being upside down and some of it in Greek she couldn't be sure.

Iannis looked down at the papers in front of him and tried to concentrate. Charlotte Manners wasn't what he'd expected. He'd hoped for a mature woman. Someone uncomplicated who would simply get on with the job of being a good doctor. How had he finished up with a charming, ultra-feminine, attractive young woman like Dr Charlotte Manners who was already making it very difficult for him to remain reserved and totally professional?

He remembered that busy morning, weeks ago, when his secretary had come into the treatment room when he'd been taking care of an emergency patient who'd fallen and gashed his leg open. Marina had had the London agency on the line, wanting to speak to him. Something about the candidate they'd chosen. As he'd already scrubbed up and put on sterile gloves, answering the phone had been the last thing he'd needed.

He remembered telling Marina that if the agency was satisfied the candidate was suitable he would abide by their decision. And then he'd got on with stitching his patient's gaping wound, knowing that he could look forward to getting some medical help for the six months from May to October when the tourists flocked over to take their summer holidays on Lirakis. The medical agency had a good reputation and he'd trusted them implicitly.

He glanced over the pages in front of him on the desk. Everything was in order. Medical school, hospital experience, all checked by the agency with impeccable references attached. Inwardly he stifled a sigh of frustration. Playing the distant unapproachable boss didn't suit him, but it was something he had to keep up as long as he could.

He remembered when Fiona had first gone back to Athens how he'd been showered with comfort from the entire female population on the island. All the women, young and old, had rallied round him, cooked him meals, made him feel welcome any time. Their doors had always been open to him but little by little he'd realised that he had to be selective.

The married women had been very correct in their behaviour and utterly faithful to their husbands, but several of the younger, unattached women had made it quite clear that they were totally available and hoping to strike up a permanent relationship with him. The unattached female tourists had been even worse, coming into the clinic with the flimsiest of excuses.

He didn't want that kind of attention. He couldn't cope with the emotional hassle that close personal relationships always brought with them. Maybe in time he would be able to forget his disastrous marriage and move on, but for the moment he simply wanted the freedom to live his own life and take care of the medical needs of the people on the island.

Iannis cleared his throat as he looked across the desk. For a moment his naturally easygoing, sympathetic nature almost revealed itself. Charlotte Manners looked tired, weary from her long journey, no doubt. He would have liked to have smiled, told her to relax, put her at her ease. But he couldn't do that. She might get the wrong idea. It was important to start as he meant to go on.

'According to your CV, your hospital career has been most successful, Dr Manners. Are you sure that you won't find it difficult to adapt to the change in working conditions?'

'As I told the agency, I'm very adaptable,' Charlotte said evenly. 'I'm thirty years old so I'm relatively mature. Over the years I've learned to cope with many kinds of medical and surgical emergencies. At my interview I was told the agency would check with you to see if I was suitable and—'

'Yes, yes, that's all been taken care of,' Iannis said brusquely.

He paused to regain his composure. OK, so Charlotte Manners was only thirty and disarmingly attractive. He hoped she would tie that luscious, long dark hair in some kind of restrictive knot at the back of her head when she worked. He could almost feel his hands stretching out to run his fingers through it. He hoped fervently that, at the very least, this disturbing woman was firmly attached to a protective boyfriend and would be longing to return to England at the end of her six-month contract.

He swallowed hard. How could he tactfully find out about her background without asking her direct questions?

'And are your relatives in England happy for you to be away from them for six months?'

'Perfectly happy.'

So she didn't want to give anything away. He knew he had no right to pursue the matter.

Charlotte watched her boss warily. No doubt he was wondering why she was here, but she wasn't going to enlighten him. Her personal life was none of his busines. She wasn't going to tell him about the way she had agonised over whether to take this job and change direction. Soon after she'd been shortlisted she'd discovered that her worst fears about James had been true. The relationship had been stale, going nowhere, she had needed to get away. Then when she had found out he was married, she had agonised no longer.

She looked across the desk. If they were going to work together, perhaps she should give her boss a tiny peek into her previous lifestyle.

'Actually, I've recently ended a relationship. I found out that my boyfriend had deceived me so this was an ideal opportunity to make a clean break and...'

As the awful memories flooded back she felt the negative emotions overwhelming her again. She couldn't go on if she was going to keep her composure. She hadn't cried before but she felt as if she might do now and this wasn't the place to do it. She scrabbled for a tissue in the bottom of her bag and blew her nose vigorously.

Iannis felt a pang of sympathy running through him. Charlotte Manners looked so sad now. The air of bravado that had surrounded her when she had arrived had completely vanished. He'd tried his hardest to remain cool but his own façade was crumbling. He pressed the intercom button on his desk and asked his secretary to bring in a cafetière and two cups.

Even as he did so he knew he would have to be very careful he didn't get any closer to her than necessary. It was extremely worrying that he was going to have to work with someone as young and lovely as the girl in front of him. She didn't look anything like thirty. More like mid-twenties! And she had an innocent, natural look about her which was very appealing. Her face was as nature had intended. No thick make-up to cover her flawless white skin. So refreshing!

Careful, Iannis! He was almost smiling as he tried to dismiss the tempting thoughts that flashed through his head. He certainly didn't want to do anything other than establish a good professional relationship with her. Romantic complications were completely out of the question. But it was difficult to quell his lustful instincts when confronted by such an attractive woman.

A couple of times during the year since Fiona had left him, he'd allowed himself to succumb to the pleasures of sleeping with an attractive woman. On both occasions he'd made sure he had been well away from Lirakis, once on holiday and once at a medical conference in Athens. He'd also insisted on a mutual understanding between them that they had been short flings with no strings attached. No past, no future, simply the no-commitment pleasures of the present.

It had been sexual release, nothing more, giving mutual enjoyment to each other. They'd parted good friends, never to meet again. Something that would be impossible here on this small island where the young women wanted marriage and babies if you so much as kissed them on the cheek!

Uncomplicated, uncommitted romance was all he could handle in the aftermath of Fiona's mind-numbing duplicity. Off the island, he could allow himself to relax, but never with a member of his staff! That was why he had to make sure that Charlotte Manners wasn't going to hear wedding bells if he took her out for the evening. Having offered the information that she'd split from her boyfriend, she would be feeling very vulnerable.

'So you're completely unnattached, Dr Manners?'

He regretted the question as soon as he'd asked it. It had come out as if he were about to proposition her. He should have wrapped it up a bit!

Charlotte's green eyes flashed. She wasn't sure where this line of questioning was leading. Dr Kimolakis was beginning to get on her nerves now that she'd recovered her composure. What was he trying to imply?

'Yes, I'm completely unnattached, as you put it,' she declared in a strong, firm, no-nonsense voice. 'Which means I'll be able to concentrate on my work here. I'm a dedicated doctor and that's the only thing I shall be interested in while I'm here on Lirakis, so…'

She broke off, knowing she'd gone too far! There was a look of alarm on Iannis Kimolakis's face now. It was the first kind of real emotion she'd seen from this difficult character. Perhaps he really was human after all.

A smart, efficient-looking, middle-aged lady came in from a door at the back of the office. She placed a tray of coffee on the desk, conversing briefly in rapid Greek with her boss. From Charlotte's limited knowledge of the language she gathered that there was a difficult patient demanding to see Dr Kimolakis as soon as possible. A nursing sister was attending to the patient and she had assessed that it wasn't urgent but she would like some back-up from the doctor.

Dr Kimolakis was frowning, explaining that he would be with the patient in a few minutes.

Charlotte sat very still, feeling terribly out of it, dreadfully tired and wishing she could simply go to her room. She was so tired she could have slept standing up!

Iannis Kimolakis poured out two cups of black coffee. Charlotte took a tentative sip and the caffeine jag revived her a little.

'I'm sorry, I shouldn't have—' she began.

'No, no, I understand.'

'You do?'

Iannis nodded solemnly as he looked across the desk into those wide green eyes. He was in real danger here, but the most dangerous part of this situation was that he didn't mind. For the first time in a year he could feel himself relaxing, letting down his guard.

He found himself drawn to glance at the envelope that had arrived from his solicitor this morning. He was free, he was finally free! The divorce was finalised. Perhaps that was why he was having these extraordinary thoughts about the woman who'd just arrived. He liked her style, the fact that she wasn't intimidated by his probably unconvincing characterisation of the stern medical director. He'd modelled himself on one of his old professors at medical school in Athens who'd been an absolute tyrant.

Don't let down your guard, his nagging inner voice told him. You're attracted to this woman and that could be even worse than finding her unattractive and scheming. Simply enjoy your freedom. Don't become involved.

Iannis cleared his throat. 'I think I should explain why I'm so interested in whether you're attached or…er, otherwise,' he began slowly.

Charlotte waited, sipping her coffee in the hope that she could stave off the weariness that threatened to overwhelm her. She noticed that Dr Kimolakis's Greek accent had become more pronounced as he had struggled to explain himself in English. Amazingly, he seemed nervous. Almost as nervous as she was. Why was he nervous? He was the boss—all the good cards were in his hand. He could send her packing if he felt like it, and probably would now that she'd shown her true colours!

'My wife and I are divorced. Since we split up I've had one or two…er…unfortunate experiences. Sometimes a comforting woman can become…how do you say it in English? A little too demanding, if you understand?'

Charlotte nodded. 'I think I know what you're getting at, but there's absolutely no—'

'Please, hear me out, Dr Manners. This isn't easy to deal with if you're working in a professional relationship with the woman involved and…' He hesitated, as if searching desperately for the right words.

'And you think professional relationships should be completely professional?'

'Exactly!' Taken off guard, Iannis flashed Charlotte a grateful smile.

Wow! Charlotte could feel the warmth of that smile heating up her increasing interest in the man. What a difference a smile made. And he had such fabulously white, evenly spaced teeth framed in that wide, inviting, sexy mouth. She tried to banish the wicked thought but her eyes remained riveted on his dark, rugged, classically high cheekboned face framed by thick, black hair which had a tendency to flop over his forehead when he moved his head.

'I entirely agree with you,' she continued in a solemn voice. 'It's not good to mix work with pleasure.'

'Absolutely not!'

'I've come out to Lirakis to work, Dr Kimolakis, and the thought of...'

The phone on the desk started ringing. 'Excuse me.' Dr Kimolakis was now frowning as he spoke in rapid Greek that was way beyond Charlotte's comprehension.

He replaced the phone and looked across the desk. 'There is a medical problem I must attend to.' He hesitated. 'Actually, if you could work with me for about half an hour in the clinic, that would help to solve the problem.'

'Now?'

'I realise that you must be tired after your long journey and that you are not officially on duty until tomorrow, but there is a difficult new male patient demanding to see me and now a female patient I've known for years has come in with a problem that needs to be resolved soon.'

Charlotte took a deep breath as she leaned forward on her chair, gripping the sides as she forced her weary mind to concentrate on the task ahead. She was a doctor first and foremost and it wasn't in her nature to avoid giving help when she was needed.

'Tell me the problem, Dr Kimolakis.'

She could see that the doctor was very worried about the female patient and her professional interest was already awakened. Even though she'd hoped to sort out the differences between them before she started working, she couldn't let a patient down.

'Sophia is forty-three who's come to the clinic for her routine antenatal examination and she is worried about having an amniocentesis which we always recommend for older mothers.'

Dr Kimolakis was standing now, making his way towards the door. 'It's simply a matter of setting her mind at rest. If you could examine her and talk to her while I see the other patient, I'll join you as soon as I can.'

Charlotte followed the doctor out into the corridor. She was aware of white walls on which several Greek landscapes had been hung.

'Tell me about Sophia.'

'I've known Sophia a long time. This is her first pregnancy at forty-three. She's worried that there may be complications because she's an older mother. I've explained it would be wise to have an amniocentesis but she's worried about the harm she thinks it might do to the baby.'

There was no time to discuss the situation any further as they arrived at the treatment room. A woman was lying on the examination couch, a white sheet pulled up over her swollen abdomen. A nurse in a white dress came forward to meet them and handed Iannis the notes.

He conversed in Greek with the nurse. 'I'll be with you in a moment, Dr Manners. Perhaps you would make a start with Sophia.'

Charlotte walked over to the patient. *'Kali mera, Sophia. Imme—'*

'Oh, you're English!' the patient exclaimed. 'I like to speak English.'

Charlotte smiled. 'I'm glad you speak English. I'm teaching myself Greek but I've still got a long way to go before I'm fluent. I'm hoping it will improve while I'm working here.'

'I love to speak English, but I'm very…how do you say it?…rusty. My parents took me to Australia for a couple of years when I was a child. I went to school there. I found it hard to settle back on the island when I returned here.'

'Why did you come back?'

The patient put one hand behind her head and raised

herself on the pillow. 'My parents got homesick and came back. I love this island, too. Gradually I got used to life here. I married my first husband when I was very young. We had a happy marriage but sadly my husband died soon afterwards.'

'That must have been difficult for you,' Charlotte said gently.

'Yes, I was alone for a long time, but then I met Karlos, the man who became my second husband.'

Sophia was smiling now.

Charlotte smiled back. 'I can see you're happy together.'

'Oh, yes! I never expected to be so happy again.'

Sophia glanced across the room at Iannis. 'May I have a look at Sophia's notes, Dr Kimolakis?'

'Of course.' Iannis handed the case notes to Charlotte. 'Thank you, Dr Manners.'

'Please, call me Charlotte.'

There was a little hesitation before he responded, 'Then you must call me Iannis.'

'Of course she must,' Sophia said. 'Everybody calls you Iannis. Why the airs and graces all of a sudden?'

Charlotte was sure that there was a flush of colour beneath Iannis's dark tan as he looked down at his patient.

'Now, don't you get difficult with me, Sophia,' he said in a bantering tone. 'Do you realise what problems I have to face if I don't keep up a professional relationship with my staff? Not to mention difficult patients like you who demand preferential treatment.'

Sophia grinned. 'Just relax, Iannis. I'm not going to scare away your new doctor.'

Iannis smiled. 'Well, if you promise to behave, I'll leave you with Charlotte while I go and see another patient.'

'Such a nice man,' Sophia said as the door closed behind Iannis. 'I've known him since I was a child. I'm glad you're here, Doctor. I always feel a bit embarrassed when Iannis examines me. I can't help it. It's the way I was brought up. My parents were very strict and old-fashioned and…well, I simply prefer not to have anyone but my husband see me undressed.'

'But he's a doctor, Sophia,' Charlotte said gently. 'It's his job to—'

'I know, but that doesn't make any difference to how I feel. And I'm afraid there are a lot of women like me on the island. Even though we all adore Iannis as a man, we married ones don't like him to see us undressed. Some of our husbands get jealous. And it doesn't help those of us like me who remember him as a child. I'm six years older than him and I can remember his mother bringing him to our house and how proud I felt to be allowed to hold the new baby.'

Sophia continued to talk about her life on the island while Charlotte was examining her. The conversation was helping her patient to relax. Occasionally Charlotte made a comment or asked a question.

'So this is your first baby, Sophia?'

'Yes, I hoped I'd get pregnant with my first husband but we were only married for a couple of years. He was a lot older than me and his health got worse and worse. Lung cancer finally took him away from me. He smoked heavily and by the time he gave up it was too late.'

'That must have been very hard for you.'

Sophia gave a barely imperceptible shrug of her shoulders under the sheet that covered her top half.

'That's life, isn't it? He was a good man. I thought I'd never love again but a couple of years ago I met my husband. He's an Australian artist who came to live on the island and paint. Iannis bought some pictures from him and they're hanging in the corridor.'

Charlotte nodded. 'I noticed them. Your husband must be very talented.'

Sophia smiled. 'Yes, he is. He's ten years younger than me. Can't think what he saw in me when he could have had his pick of the younger women on the island.'

Charlotte smiled as she reached for a pair of forceps to take a vaginal swab. 'It's all turned out for the best, hasn't it?'

'It certainly has.'

Charlotte finished her examination and, stripping off her gloves, went over to the sink to wash her hands before sitting down on the chair next to the examination couch. Sophia, buttoning up her loose cotton dress, was sitting up, leaning against the pillows.

'Everything's progressing well, Sophia. Your most recent ultrasound scan showed no detectable abnormality but—'

'I know what you're going to say, Charlotte, and the answer is still no. Iannis has advised me to have an amniocentesis because I'm forty-three and therefore could be at risk of a Down's syndrome or spina bifida baby and various other things Iannis has explained to me. But I've talked it over with Karlos and I've decided I shall love this baby whatever it's like. I've waited all my life to be a mother and nobody's going to stop me bearing my own child.' Sophia's voice had risen to a crescendo.

Charlotte leaned forward and took hold of her patient's hand. 'Sophia, nobody wants to stop you having the baby. Nobody is suggesting that—'

Someone knocked on the door. She could hear Iannis asking if he might come in.

'Of course.' Charlotte felt a deep sense of relief that she wasn't going to have to tackle the problem by herself.

Iannis came over to the couch and looked down at their patient. 'Sophia, we're only trying to help you.'

'You can't help me. My cousin had a Down's syndrome child when she was forty-five. She loves that little girl. I would prefer to have a child like that than no child.'

'Sophia, there's an excellent chance you will have a perfect child,' Iannis said gently. 'But wouldn't you rather go through your pregnancy with peace of mind knowing that was the case? I know you've told me you're worried, so why don't we try to set your mind at rest?'

Charlotte was impressed by Iannis's calm tone, his air of total caring. He was not at all as she'd imagined—thank goodness! Underneath the stern façade he'd put on when she'd first arrived, he was a very emotional man. She could see how worried he was on his patient's behalf.

Sophia's frown deepened. 'I read somewhere that amniocentesis can sometimes harm the baby.'

'Yes, very rarely this has been the case,' Iannis said calmly. 'But more recently—'

'No, Iannis,' Sophia said, heaving herself to her feet.

Charlotte put out a hand to steady her. 'Sophia, amniocentesis is not the only test you could take. There is another non-invasive test that—'

'What does that mean, non-invasive?'

'It means having a simple blood test and—'

'I don't need it and I'm going home now,' Sophia said firmly.

'Sophia…' Iannis began, but his patient was already at the door.

Sophia turned to look at them. 'I don't want to sound ungrateful, but I'll have this baby as my mother and my grandmother did, over in my cottage by the sea. My cousin will help to deliver it. She's had six babies of her own. The first five were perfect and so is the sixth. She's simply different to the others.'

Iannis drew in his breath. 'May I come over to see you, Sophia? Perhaps if we talk about—'

'Yes, you can come over. You can talk till you're blue in the face, Iannis, but I won't change my mind.'

As the door slammed behind their patient, Iannis and Charlotte looked at each other.

'I'm really worried about Sophia,' Iannis said, quietly. 'She's a very stubborn woman. When she says she's opting out of the system she means it.'

'Iannis, I hope I didn't put her off. I was—'

'No, of course you didn't. I was interested in your idea of doing a blood serum screening. That was what you were referring to, wasn't it?'

Charlotte nodded. 'I think it would be a good alternative if we could talk Sophia round.'

'It's worth a try, but we need to remember that—' He broke off. 'Charlotte, you look exhausted.'

Iannis's warm, concerned tone, so different to the cold, impersonal voice he'd used when they'd first met, was extremely disturbing in the nicest possible way.

'Yes, I'm pretty tired. I think—'

'I think you should be in bed.'

She loved the way he said the word 'bed', making it sound like the cosy haven it would be if she were snuggled up next to an attractive hunk like Iannis Kimolakis! She found herself wondering what it would be like if she were to follow through such an outrageous fantasy.

She told herself sternly to stop fantasising and get some sleep. She was feeling positively light-headed from the lack of it. That was why she was having these ridiculous thoughts.

'If you'll give me directions to my quarters, I'll be on my way,' she said primly.

'It's quite simple. If you go back to my office, my secretary will give you a diagram of the medical complex. And now, if you'll excuse me, I must go back to my patient. I've had to admit him because the problem is more complicated than I'd thought.'

'I didn't know you had in-patients.'

'Yes, we have several beds. This patient has been transferred from our private health and fitness section. He tore a ligament in his knee when he slipped off the treadmill in the gym. He's threatening to sue, which would be most unfortunate.'

Iannis was already walking away down the corridor. Charlotte noticed that the tenderness she'd imagined in his voice had vanished completely. He was totally and utterly professional again, simply handing her over to his secretary so that he could get on with more important matters.

She remembered reading about the health and fitness section of the clinic when she'd applied for this job. Apparently it was very popular with tourists who needed a complete break to get themselves fit or simply relax. It sounded like a leisure centre with some relaxation and yoga classes for those who wanted them. She was interested in the project and looking forward to checking it out—but not now!

All she wanted to do now was find her room, pull off her clothes and climb between the sheets. She would sleep until tomorrow so that she was fit to face up to the challenge of working with Dr Iannis Kimolakis.

It would indeed be a real challenge, for more reasons than she cared to think about at the present moment.

CHAPTER TWO

'I HOPE your boss realises I'm going to make things very difficult for him.'

The irate patient's frown deepened as he stared up at Charlotte. She'd felt nervous on this her first morning at the clinic as she'd reported for duty, so dealing with this obstreperous man was calling for a great deal of patience. If she'd been working in her London hospital she'd have been surrounded by colleagues. But there hadn't been a nurse in sight and she had no idea where her boss had spirited himself off to at this crucial time.

She noticed that her patient was actually trembling with rage as he spat out his angry words. It was becoming increasingly difficult to remain impassive as she continued to replace the dressing on Richard Horton's injured knee.

'Dr Kimolakis is aware of your concern, Mr Horton, and—'

'Iannis hasn't even been in to see me this morning. What kind of an establishment are you running here? If I'd known I was going to be stuck here in the back of beyond—Ah! there you are, Iannis.'

Iannis closed the door behind him and moved with studied calm over to the bed.

'So what are you going to do about my injuries, eh? I hardly slept a wink last night. The room's too small. The air-conditioning is pathetic. I've asked for a bigger room with—'

'Mr Horton,' Iannis interrupted. 'Everything is under control. I'm having you transferred to hospital in Athens on the morning ferry, leaving in one hour's time. One of my nurses is going with you. You'll be taken by ambulance to the hospital and the surgeon, who is a personal friend of mine, will then assess your injury.'

The patient seemed mollified somewhat by the firm, authoritarian tone of the doctor.

'And then what? What will happen to me?'

'You'll most likely have a meniscectomy operation to removed the torn ligaments. That will effectively repair your injured knee. I've just been speaking on the phone to my colleague in Athens and he assures me that he will give your case priority and, if he considers you are a suitable case, he will perform keyhole surgery.'

Richard frowned. 'Is that a good idea, Doctor?'

'It's an excellent idea. I used to be a surgeon in the hospital where you'll be treated and I've worked alongside the surgeon who will be doing your operation. With expert keyhole surgery the wound will be minimal and you'll therefore be able to come back here for convalescence much sooner. Alternatively, we could have you transferred back to England direct from hospital in Athens.'

Richard leaned back against his pillows. 'No, I'd like to come back here,' he said quietly, averting his eyes so that he was now staring towards the window where the view of the surrounding hills was spectacularly beautiful in the morning sunlight.

'I came here because I was stressed out,' the patient continued quietly. 'So far your so-called health and fitness section has made me even more stressed.' He hesitated. 'But, nevertheless, in spite of everything that's happened, I'd like to give you a chance to prove yourselves by spending more time here.'

'I'm surprised you want to return here,' Charlotte put in evenly. 'You were telling me just now that you couldn't wait to get away from here and that you were going to contact your solicitor.'

'Well, I've changed my mind. Now that it looks as if you're actually going to do something for me, I'll give you another chance. But I really think you should do something about that treadmill. I shouldn't have fallen off like that.'

'No, you shouldn't,' Charlotte said, handing over a cup of black coffee from the tray which a nurse had just placed on the patient's bedside table. 'What do you usually take in your coffee, Mr Horton? Milk, sugar or perhaps…?'

Charlotte's hand was hovering over the half-empty whisky bottle secreted in the bedside drawer that her patient had been trying to close when she'd first arrived. From the fumes on her patient's breath as she'd dressed his knee she'd gathered that a fair amount had been consumed that morning. If Richard Horton drank throughout the day it was no wonder he'd fallen off the treadmill.

The implication hung in the air. Charlotte, one eyebrow slightly raised questioningly, looked across the bed at Iannis. His eyes met hers and she thought she detected an expression of approval but she couldn't be sure. She hadn't seen him since yesterday. Although she'd wakened in the night feeling apprehensive about working with him this morning she knew she needn't have worried.

Richard gave a nervous cough. 'I don't usually drink so early in the day but under the exceptional circumstances I thought that—'

Iannis removed the bottle before Richard Horton could reach for it.

'That's not a good idea, Richard. You're on powerful painkillers which don't mix with alcohol. As I recall, one of the problems you wanted to sort out while you were here with us in the health and fitness section was your excessive consumption of alcohol. So, don't you think it would be a good idea to start now?'

Richard closed his eyes and groaned. 'Hell, I'm in such a mess, aren't I?'

Charlotte leaned over her patient and took hold of his hand. 'You're going to get better, Richard. If you just put yourself in our hands, we'll do all we can to get you fit and well again.'

The patient opened his eyes and looked up in surprise at Charlotte. Her quiet, sympathetic tone wasn't something he often experienced. He'd heard one of the nurses describing him as overbearing and difficult to deal with. He couldn't think why. Perhaps it was because he'd been feeling lousy for such a long time.

'OK, you win,' he said slowly. 'I came out here to search for a miracle cure. I haven't felt good for months now. The doctors at home can't find anything wrong with me—apart from the drinking, which is the only thing that's been holding me together—so they suggested I try to get myself in better shape. I've been trying to lose weight but…well, I'd like to carry on with my regime to get fit but now that I've hurt my knee…'

'That will soon be fixed at the hospital,' Iannis said quickly. 'When you get back here we'll devise a special health and fitness regime for you.'

'That's what I need.' Richard hesitated again. 'You know, one of the problems is that I'm not used to taking orders from other people. I've been running my own company and not being in charge isn't easy for me. Still, I don't mind being kept in check by a charming young doctor like Charlotte.'

'I'll ask the nurse to pack your bag.' Iannis said quickly. 'The clinic car will be ready for you in a few minutes.'

'Thanks, Iannis. Thanks, Charlotte...may I call you Charlotte?'

'Of course, if I can call you Richard.'

The patient smiled. 'Friends?'

'Of course.'

Outside in the corridor, Iannis put his hand on her arm. 'I'm glad you were there, Charlotte. You certainly charmed our patient.'

'A woman's touch. That's what was needed.'

Iannis gave her a wry grin. 'Is that what it was? In that case will you bring your magic touch with you and help me sort out Sophia's problem? She's nearly sixteen weeks pregnant so we can't leave it any longer.'

'Is Sophia here at the clinic again?'

'No, we'll have to go over to her house and see her.'

'Does she know we're coming?'

'Of course not! She won't be too pleased to see us. That's why I'd like you to come with me.'

'Coward!'

Suddenly, Charlotte realised that she was gaining the upper hand in this professional relationship. Her boss was almost deferring to her. He was probably as apprehensive about working with her as she was with him. She felt a surge of sympathy for him. He'd been the only doctor in the clinic and patients were often difficult. Especially the fee-paying ones from the health and fitness section. It didn't matter how well qualified and experienced you were if the patients wouldn't co-operate.

'So where does Sophia live?' Charlotte quickened her pace to keep up with her boss.

Iannis paused outside the door to his office. 'Not too far away. Meet me here in half an hour. I've already seen the patients who required my attention this morning. If anybody else arrives who can't be dealt with by one of the nurses I'll get a call on my mobile for advice. Then we can deal with them when we get back.'

'I can't get used to the relaxed, peaceful atmosphere that seems to pervade the clinic,' Charlotte said, looking out of the open window of the Jeep at the stunningly beautiful landscape as they rolled along over the hill.

'Relaxed? You think it's relaxed?'

Iannis took his eyes off the road for a moment, slowing down as he turned to look at her. 'I suppose the Greeks are a very relaxed people. Here on Lirakis we're not so…how do you say it in English?…so frenetic, so rushing about, but that doesn't mean we don't get the work done. We might get it done tomorrow instead of today, but that's OK. Medical emergencies are different, however. When there's an emergency, we can get things done faster than anybody.'

Charlotte heard the note of pride in his voice. 'I think I'm going to enjoy working here.'

'I hope so, Charlotte.'

She liked the husky tone of his voice. What was even more likable was the way he took one hand off the steering-wheel and placed it over hers.

'I certainly hope so, Charlotte,' he began again, his hand sending shivers over her skin. 'Because I really need someone to help me. Lately, I've felt very alone at the clinic.'

Quickly he put his hand back on the wheel wondering, as he did so, what on earth had inspired him to make such a gesture! And why had he made the confession that he felt lonely? That was the last thing he should have said. If she was anything like the other unattached women he'd encountered recently, she'd take that as a definite come-on sign.

He slowed down to allow a couple of goats to amble across the track, the bells around their necks tinkling as they took their time to reach the other side and clamber over the wall.

As soon as they'd disappeared, he put his foot down hard on the clutch to negotiate the narrow bend that led over the bumpy stones down to the little bay where Sophia lived. He reflected that yesterday he'd tried so hard to put on the stern doctor act but today he was undoing all that. Letting down his guard with Charlotte wasn't going to help. What on earth had got into him, apart from the fact that he found her extremely attractive? More than that, he found her intensely desirable if he was really truthful and that would be his downfall if he didn't check his feelings.

'I'll fill you in on the case,' he said quickly, trying to adopt a brisk, professional tone. 'I've known Sophia all my life.'

'I know,' Charlotte said quietly. 'She told me she remembers you as a baby.'

Iannis skidded to a halt on the sandy track and turned off the engine. He opened his door but remained still sitting with one hand on the wheel as he looked at the woman he was finding it so difficult to maintain a professional relationship with. The sound of the waves and the feel of the sun on his back was making it doubly hard to remain cool and focused on the task in hand. He felt a sudden mad urge to suggest they throw off their clothes and run naked into the sea, swimming out to a small rocky island where they could bask in the sun and perhaps…

He cleared his throat. 'Yes, Sophia likes to talk about how our mothers were friends and she used to take care of me when the mothers were chatting.'

'You said your mothers were friends. Are they still friends or…?'

'My mother died when I was very small. My grandmother raised me. She died last year.'

'How sad! I'm sorry. And your father?'

'After my mother died, my father went to America, to seek his fortune as they say in all the fictitious adventure stories.'

Iannis was smiling now. 'I remember how proud I was when my father took me on his knee and told me he was going to make himself fabulously wealthy. Everybody in America was rich. When he'd made enough money he was going to come back and collect me. Take me over to America to live in his big house with him. I would swim all day in his swimming pool and…'

He broke off and leaned back against the seat. A large white seagull had landed on the bonnet of the Jeep. Close to the windscreen, its head on one side, it was plainly intrigued by the people inside. Charlotte waited quietly, watching Iannis as he relived what must have been a poignant experience for a young boy.

She could imagine the scenario, the proud little boy sitting on his father's lap, gazing up at him with admiration. And she could see in her mind's eye just how handsome Iannis would have looked even as a child. His dark brown eyes would have been dancing with excitement at the prospect of going overseas with his soon-to-be-rich, successful father.

She leaned across and put her hand on Iannis's bare arm, just below the place where he'd rolled up his white cotton sleeve. His skin felt warm and damp. She could feel the dark hairs against her fingers.

'And did you go to America?' she asked gently.

Iannis shook his head sadly. 'No, I never saw my father again. He got a job as a taxi driver in New York. Soon after he started work he was involved in a fatal car crash on the highway outside the city. A multiple pile-up. He didn't stand a chance, apparently.'

'How awful for you!'

'My grandmother didn't tell me for a while. Not until she thought I was old enough to understand.' He hesitated. 'It kind of…it kind of makes you tough when your dreams are shattered.'

She squeezed his arm in sympathy. He put his hand over hers, holding her fingers against him, oh, so gently.

'I don't know why I'm telling you all this,' he said huskily.

'Probably because I always ask too many questions,' she said gently, as she removed her hand and sat upright once more, looking out of the windscreen at the inquisitive seagull. The emotional tension between them was palpable. This wasn't what she'd planned for the first day of her new life. This was a situation she was trying desperately to avoid. So she'd better start to tread more carefully.

She could feel her heart beating rapidly as she took a deep breath to try to bring her emotions under control.

'Do you know, Iannis, I really believe that seagull understands what we're saying?'

Iannis laughed and the tension was broken. 'I think you're right. Let's go and see Sophia.'

'You were telling me about her case history.'

'Well, briefly, at forty-three, Sophia is scared because she's described as an "at risk" mother. She'd like to know if her baby is normal. The ultrasound revealed no abnormality. Ideally, we should do an amniocentesis but she's worried it might harm the baby when a needle is inserted into her womb to draw out a sample of the amniotic fluid.'

'In that case, I think we should try to convince her that a non-invasive test would solve the problem, don't you, Iannis?'

Iannis nodded. 'But we have to remember that something

like blood serum screening is not as conclusive as an amniocentesis.'

'It's better than no test at all, don't you think? And we need to keep tabs on Sophia. Her idea that she should have her baby out here with the help of an untrained cousin might have been OK years ago when it was accepted that some babies wouldn't survive, but at Sophia's age and—'

'Yes, yes, I'm not disputing that. I entirely agree that we need to keep her under our wing until we've delivered this baby. So let's go and see if we can get back into her confidence again. I'm sure you can exert some of your charm on her, Charlotte.'

Having leapt down onto the stony track, Iannis was now holding out his arms towards her to help in her descent from the high-chassied Jeep.

She held onto her feelings as she allowed his strong arms to grip her around the waist and lift her down. They were standing very close. Charlotte drew in her breath. Having made such an effort to start afresh, why did she now find herself in the arms of a man she hardly knew? Men were not to be trusted. She could do without the hassle they invariably brought with them.

She glanced up at the dark brown eyes looking down at her. Was that expression half-mocking? Was Iannis Kimolakis so sure of his attraction that he considered she would be a pushover?

She moved away quickly. 'Which way?' she asked, her tone as abrupt and cool as she could make it.

'Along the path here.' As Iannis led the way he was trying to calm his turbulent emotions.

Moments ago, as he'd helped Charlotte down from the Jeep, he'd tried so hard to remain completely unmoved by the feel of her body. His hands on her waist had been itching to caress the smooth white skin beneath the short sexy top she was wearing. It had been difficult not to pull her towards him for a long, sensual kiss. Those luscious lips that had been upturned towards his had seemed to be asking if a kiss would destroy the fine balance of emotion that was running between them.

No! He was imagining things! Charlotte had no interest in him as a man. She'd merely been polite. Grateful that he'd helped her down from the high passenger seat. She was a tall woman but it was a long way down to the ground. And her voice, asking the way, had been cold, frosty almost. He knew he had to watch his step.

One, he didn't want to have another relationship for a long time because he needed to keep his freedom until the Fiona scars had healed over. Two, Charlotte herself was suffering from the trauma of a disastrous relationship. The two of them together would be like a pair of wounded seagulls washed up on an alien shore, unaware of the approaching waves that were threatening to engulf them.

He strode purposefully forward along the coastal path that led to Sophia's cottage.

'We're here!' A little later Iannis stood with his hand on a large boulder at the side of the track that snaked round to the next bay.

Charlotte looked at the small cottage overshadowed by high cliffs. She paused for a moment to listen to the crashing of the waves on the shore and the call of the gulls.

'It's very beautiful but it's a very isolated spot. Not even a road up to the cottage. Only this narrow sandy path.'

Iannis smiled. 'That's how Sophia and Karlos like to live. As you know, he's an artist and Sophia…well, she's a pure romantic. She waited a long time to find the right man. Her first husband was a quiet, down-to-earth man, kind and considerate but not the sort of man to raise Sophia's pulse rate.'

The path had broadened out. Large, smooth pebbles from the shore had been arranged at the edges to form a low wall that had small tubs of geraniums built into the sides. Charlotte fell into step beside Iannis.

'Do you think Karlos raises Sophia's pulse rate?' she asked, raising her eyes towards Iannis.

'Oh, yes! They're like two young lovers. Sophia told me this was what she'd waited for all her life.'

Charlotte paused for a moment. They were within a stone's throw of the cottage now. 'Sophia told me that Karlos was a lot younger than her.'

Iannis stopped walking and turned to look down at Charlotte. 'Yes, ten years. But in the first flush of their marriage together it doesn't seem to matter. Especially now that Sophia is going to have their baby. This is why I'm hoping and praying that there won't be any complications with the pregnancy and delivery.'

'Sophia told me that she couldn't think why Karlos should have chosen her instead of all the younger women he could have had.'

For a moment Iannis looked worried. 'She said the same thing to me. I don't know much about Karlos except that his parents were Greeks who went to live in Australia before he was born. He's a charming man. If he were ever to leave her…'

Charlotte shivered. 'Doesn't bear thinking about, does it?'

'Oh, Sophia would cope, just like she's coped with all the other disappointments in her life. Let's hope it will never come to that.'

The door was wide open and from inside the cottage came the sound of background music. Ethnic, Greek or Turkish, the haunting strains of a bazouka, a tambourine and a high-pitched flute. A recording probably because it was snapped off as soon as Iannis tapped on the door.

'Yassoo, Sophia!'

Sophia came through a beaded doorway from the kitchen. She stared at Iannis and Charlotte.

'Ah, I might have known. I expected you'd come to see me but I hoped you'd leave it a bit longer. I haven't changed my mind so…'

Iannis stepped inside. 'Sophia, we can't leave it much longer. You're almost sixteen weeks and we have to resolve the question of which test to use. May I come in?'

Sophia shrugged. 'Since when have you ever needed an invitation, Iannis?' She hesitated. 'Well, now that you're here I'll call Karlos. He's in the garden at the back here. Go and sit on the front terrace.'

Iannis retraced his steps and joined Charlotte on the sunlit terrace overlooking the sea. The bright sun was dancing on the waves. There wasn't a cloud in the sky. An idyllic spot. Charlotte found herself praying once more that they would be able to deliver a healthy baby.

As she sank down onto one of the rustic seats that surrounded the roughly hewn wooden table she reflected that Sophia's baby would be due some time towards the end of her own contract here on Lirakis at the end of October.

A tall, good-looking, dark-haired, suntanned man in his early thirties come out through the open door of the cottage carrying a large bottle in one hand and three glasses in the other. He had a very striking appearance, the sort of man who would make a flamboyant entrance when he went into a room full of people. By contrast, Sophia, determined as she was to go her own way, was a much quieter person.

She followed her husband carrying a tray on which there were small dishes of olives, some taramasalata and a dish which Charlotte recognised as dolmades, the small parcels of rice wrapped in vine leaves that she'd so enjoyed when she'd spent that holiday in Greece long ago with her parents. There was also a mug of tea, which was obviously for Sophia.

'Hello, I'm Karlos.' The tall man put down the bottle and glasses on the table and extended his hand towards Charlotte.

'I'm Charlotte.'

'Welcome! So you've come to check how we live in our simple rustic life,' Karlos said, his Australian accent making it obvious that he hadn't lived very long in Greece. 'Iannis, you don't need to worry about Sophia. She's as fit as a girl half her age.'

Karlos was pouring the straw-coloured wine into the tall glasses. 'Retsina OK for you folks?'

'Fine!' Iannis said.

Charlotte took a tentative sip. The first taste scorched the back of her throat. She held off for a few seconds and tried again. That was better. Yes, retsina was definitely an acquired taste.

Karlos was watching her, a wry grin on his face. 'You don't have to drink your retsina, Doc. I can make you a cup of tea if you prefer.'

'No. It has a very distinctive taste and…I'm determined to try everything once while I'm out here.'

Both men laughed and Charlotte found herself blushing. 'Within reason,' she said primly, putting down her glass.

'Well, now,' she continued evenly, as she tried to regain her composure, 'Iannis and I have come to explain about the options for tests that Sophia can have. If you really don't want to have an amniocentesis you could have blood serum screening.'

'What's that?' Karlos asked, frowning.

'It's non-invasive. A sample of blood is taken and sent

away for analysis. Three substances in the blood are measured to indicate the chances of possible handicap and assess its type,' Charlotte continued.

'What kind of handicap?' Karlos asked, reaching for his wife's hand.

Iannis cleared his throat. 'Well, if there was low alpha fetoprotein in the blood, it might indicate Down's syndrome, for example.'

'But if the blood sample was shown to have none of the risk factors, your chances of having a Down's syndrome baby would be less than one in two hundred and fifty.'

'But you couldn't be absolutely sure even then, could you?' Sophia said in a small voice. 'I'd rather not—'

'No, darling, I think you should go ahead and have the blood test. I'd like to know as much about our baby before he's born as possible.' Karlos turned to look at Iannis. 'I mean, how much information can this test give?'

Iannis leaned forward. 'The test can detect two out of three Down's babies and four out of five spina bifida cases. However, a negative result would indicate that it's highly unlikely your baby would be disabled.'

'But it's not one hundred per cent conclusive, is it?' Sophia said. 'I'm going to love my baby whether it's healthy or not.'

Charlotte patted Sophia's hand. 'Of course you are, Sophia. But if the test gave an indication there was a problem, we would all be more prepared to cope with the birth and the care of your baby afterwards. On the other hand, as we've already pointed out, if the test gives a negative result, that would mean that the baby is likely to be perfectly healthy.'

Karlos put his arm around his wife's shoulders. 'Darling, I really think we should find out all we can about our baby.

We'd then know if he's likely to be healthy or if there is a problem we should prepare ourselves for.'

A faint smile flickered across Sophia's face. 'Oh, so it's a boy, is it?'

Karlos grinned. 'I don't care if it's a kangaroo so long as it's our baby, darling. So just take the blood test and then we can all be prepared. We'll either know that everything is likely to be normal, or, if a handicap has been detected, we'll be ready to cope with it. Think positive darling. We're going to love our baby, whatever it's like.' Karlos turned to look at Iannis and Charlotte. 'Don't worry, I'll talk Sophia round. When can she have the test?'

'There's a very small window for this test,' Iannis said. 'The patient should be sixteen to eighteen weeks pregnant so next week would be ideal for Sophia. And we could give you the results in about ten days' time.'

'Fine! Monday morning OK, Doc?'

Iannis smiled at Karlos. 'Absolutely.'

'You know it makes sense, darling,' Karlos said, putting his arm round his wife. 'You've got nothing to lose and it'll set your mind at rest. I'll take you along to the clinic and—'

'Oh, I suppose so, if you really want me to, Karlos.'

Karlos smiled. 'I do. So set that up for Monday morning, Iannis.'

'Fine. We'll be waiting and—Excuse me a moment.'

Iannis took his mobile phone from the pocket of his stone-coloured cotton trousers.

Charlotte watched him as he spoke rapidly to the caller. His face held a serious expression. From her elementary Greek she gathered that there was some kind of emergency at the clinic. She began to prepare herself for an imminent departure.

Iannis cut the connection and looked across the table towards her.

'That was Nurse Adriana. A five-year-old boy has been brought in with an injury to the throat. We'd better go back at once.'

Charlotte was already standing. 'We'll see you on Monday morning, Sophia.'

'Maybe I—' Sophia began, as her resolve weakened, but her husband was adamant.

'We'll be there,' he said, putting his arm around his wife's shoulders once more.

'So tell me about this throat injury,' Charlotte said as the Jeep hurtled along over the rough track.

'Apparently, the boy was climbing up the garden gate. He'd reached the top when he fell, gashing himself on the large metal lock. Adriana says his throat is slit from ear to ear because he must have turned his head as the lock tore his skin.'

Charlotte swallowed hard as she had a momentary vision of what might have happened. She wondered if any major artery was involved.

'Is the bleeding arterial?' she asked quickly.

'Fortunately not, but it's a very long scar. He didn't injure his windpipe so his breathing is OK. But we'll need to give him a general anaesthetic before we can suture such an extensive wound.'

'I've had experience in anaesthetics,' Charlotte said.

'I know. That was one of the qualifications I asked the agency to insist on. I don't often need to use a general anaesthetic but this is one of the occasions where it will be essential.'

Iannis was slowing the Jeep now as they went down the hill that led to the clinic. Charlotte could see the holidaymakers in the next bay to the village, enjoying the bright sunshine on the beach and in the sea. She thought about the little boy lying bewildered and frightened in the clinic.

'Five years old, you said?'

Iannis nodded as he drove through the clinic gates.

'Poor little mite.' Charlotte's hand was on the passenger door. 'Let's go and see what we can do.'

Charlotte took hold of the little boy's hand. '*Posseleni?* What's your name?'

Terrified eyes gazed up at her but the boy didn't speak for a few seconds. Then very quietly he said, *'Imme Vasilis.'*

Vasilis's distraught mother had moved away to sit by the wall when the two doctors had arrived. She was holding back the tears as she asked if her little boy was going to be all right. Apparently she'd locked the gate to prevent him going out and getting dirty while she got ready to take him over to the town for some shopping. She began weeping. If only she hadn't locked the gate!

Iannis was doing his best to comfort the mother. Telling her it couldn't have been helped. That these things happened to little boys. Vasilis was out of danger now that he was here at the clinic.

Charlotte removed the large sterile pad Adriana had placed over the cut, quickly replacing it with another and holding it in place to staunch the flow of blood. Iannis joined her to assess the damage.

'It's a miracle that an artery wasn't severed,' Iannis whispered to Charlotte.

Charlotte swallowed hard as she tried to remain utterly professional. Where small children were concerned she found it very difficult to remain detached. Their helplessness tugged at her heartstrings and the grief of the mother was almost unbearable to witness. She could imagine how she would feel if this were her child.

'We're going to send you to sleep, Vasilis,' Iannis said gently. 'And while you're asleep we'll mend that cut for you. You've been such a brave boy.'

He turned to look at Vasilis's mother. 'We're going to take Vasilis into our operating theatre, Tatiana. You can wait here or go home, whichever you—'

'I'll stay,' Tatiana said, moving across to kiss her little boy. 'I'll be here when you wake up, Vasilis.'

It was a small operating theatre, little more than a treatment room really, but a swift look around had assured Charlotte that there was everything necessary for minor operations. Suturing a deep cut that had only just missed being an arterial disaster was well within their capabilities once their small patient had been anaesthetised.

Charlotte put in the IV line and as the morphine began to take effect Vasilis mumbled, 'You said I was going to sleep but I don't feel...I really don't want to sleep...I want to go home because...well...you see...'

Charlotte looked across the table at Iannis. 'He's out now.'

She fixed the breathing apparatus and checked the cylinders before telling Iannis he could go ahead.

It was a painstaking operation. The delicate layers of tissue beneath the skin had to be sutured first. Each stitch was a challenge. In between checking her little patient's breathing, Charlotte helped Iannis, passing him sutures, swabs and instruments as required. It was a full two hours before the final external stitch was in place.

Iannis stood back to get a better look at his handiwork.

'Beautiful embroidery, if I may say so!' Charlotte said.

Iannis smiled and the tension eased for the first time since they'd started the operation.

'My grandmother taught me how to sew when I was very small. I don't think she knew just how useful it was going to be in later life. Although I have to say this is one of the worst cuts I've had to deal with. Vasilis will have a large scar that's not going to fade for a long time, if at all. However neat you try to be, the scar is always visible.'

'I should think he'll get a lot of street cred from his mates at school. They'll all be very impressed that he survived such a horrific accident.'

'Yes, he's a plucky little boy.' Iannis peeled off his surgical gloves and tossed them in the bin. 'Let's get him back to the room Adriana has prepared for him.'

'I'll stay with him until he's fully conscious,' Charlotte said.

'And then?' Iannis asked.

Charlotte looked at Iannis questioningly, unsure of what he meant. 'And then I'll leave him with Adriana and carry on with my work here. What else is likely to happen today?'

'No further emergencies, I hope. We could probably finish in time for a drink at the taverna if you'd like to join me at the end of the afternoon.'

Iannis was keeping his tone deliberately cool, telling himself that he was merely being hospitable to the newest recruit on his staff. It was the least he could do as a welcome to someone who was miles away from home.

Charlotte hesitated, but only momentarily. She knew it made sense to make friends with her boss on a social level. 'Yes, I'd like that.'

A perfectly logical reaction, she assured herself. Two professionals having a drink together at the end of the day. What could be more normal and ordinary?

Why, then, was her pulse beginning to race at a furious pace? Watch it! She didn't need any kind of emotional hassle. It was too soon. She wasn't ready for any kind of emotional excitement. She mustn't rush things. Just take it easy for a while…

CHAPTER THREE

SITTING at a table outside the taverna, looking out across the bay, Charlotte was feeling more relaxed than she'd felt for a long time. Iannis raised his glass towards her.

They clinked glasses. Charlotte watched, fascinated, as the ice cubes turned the clear ouzo into a cloudy liquid. She took a sip of her own drink and couldn't help herself from coughing loudly.

Iannis smiled. 'Is this the first time you've tried ouzo, Charlotte?'

Charlotte nodded as she tried hard to swallow the fiery liquid. 'I was too young to drink when I was last on a Greek island. I'll treat this drink with caution. Maybe I'll have an orange juice next time…I mean, that is…'

She squirmed inwardly. Iannis had probably intended this meeting to be a one-off welcome drink for a new colleague. Talk about making herself available for the evening! It must have been the ouzo that was making her throw caution to the winds.

'I've got plenty of time if you have,' Iannis said easily. 'The staff at the clinic phone me on my mobile when they need me. I'll drop into the clinic later this evening to check on Vasilis, but I don't think there'll be a problem the nurses can't handle.'

'He was remarkably well when I left him. His mother and Adriana were watching over him and dancing attendance every time he raised a finger.'

Iannis smiled. 'Tatiana's a good mother. I've known her since we were at school together.'

Charlotte swirled the cubes of ice around in her glass. 'You must know almost everybody on the island.'

Iannis nodded. 'All except the tourists who come and go before I've really had time to get to know them. The tourists are the reason I need a doctor from England to help me out.'

He pushed the bowl containing olives, small pieces of cucumber, slices of tomato and little cubes of feta cheese doused in a vinaigrette dressing across the table towards her.

Charlotte picked up a small fork and helped herself to a piece of the soft, white, tangy feta cheese. It crumbled deliciously on her tongue.

'How long have you been the only doctor on the island?'

Iannis leaned back against the wooden chair, stretching his long legs in front of him. The sole of one of his shoes touched Charlotte's sandals.

'Sorry!' He moved his chair backwards, turning sideways so that he could stretch out more easily.

'That's OK,' Charlotte said quickly. She waited for Iannis to answer her question.

'There's another doctor in the town. He's lived here all his life. Dr Pachos is in his sixties now and theoretically retired. He was my doctor when I was a child—in fact, he often likes to remind me that he brought me into the world.'

Iannis smiled. 'I used to think it was so he could keep me in my place but I think he's just nostalgic about the old days. Nothing has changed in his surgery for years. It's still the same cosy old room at the back of his house. People drop in for a chat with him if they're not feeling well. But mostly they come here to the clinic to see me.'

'It's a rough road over the hill to the clinic.'

'There's a new road that skirts around the hill, slightly

longer but better for vehicles. So it's a quick way here if you've got one of the few cars on the island.'

'I don't think I'll aspire to a car in the short time I'm going to be here.'

'You can always borrow mine if you're called out to see a patient.'

Charlotte smiled. 'Thanks very much. Tell me, Iannis, as the only doctor working full time on Lirakis, don't you find it very hard work, especially during the summer when the tourists arrive?'

Iannis's brow furrowed. 'There was another doctor, who left a year ago,' he said, quietly. 'My wife.'

'Ah, I see.' Charlotte didn't, but she hoped that Iannis would explain.

He rocked back on his chair, lifting his hand to attract the attention of a waiter who was sitting outside the door of the taverna. The waiter came across and poured more ouzo into Iannis's glass. Charlotte shook her head in answer to the waiter's query.

Iannis drank deeply before setting the glass down on the table, staring out beyond the bay to where the sun was sinking towards the water.

Charlotte looked in the same direction, marvelling at the beautiful colours of the sunset and the pink- and gold-tinged clouds that threatened to obscure the fiery ball before it dipped beneath the horizon. She hoped that the clouds would hold back until nightfall so that the splendour of the sunset could be fully appreciated and admired.

She was secretly hoping that Iannis would enlighten her about his mysterious wife. Why had she gone away from this idyllic island? Why had she left her handsome husband?

As if reading her thoughts, Iannis began to speak in a low, husky voice.

'Fiona and I were born here on Lirakis. We both left the island at the same time to go to medical school in Athens together and married as soon as we were qualified.'

Iannis gave a deep sigh. 'The marriage didn't work out. Fiona left me.'

As Charlotte listened to the stark facts that Iannis revealed in a quiet, unemotional voice, she knew there must be a lot more to it than that but it wasn't her place to pry. Maybe when she got to know Iannis better he would open up and tell her more. But for the moment she could see that was all she was going to get.

'I'm sorry your marriage broke up,' she said gently. 'That must have been—'

'It was inevitable!'

Charlotte was surprised at Iannis's vehement tone but she made no comment.

'We should never have married, not when…'

His voice trailed away and he remained silent for a few moments.

'We both worked at the hospital where we trained in Athens. When we'd had a few years' experience, we came back here to the place where we'd both been born. Dr Pachos had contacted me. He told me that the tourists were arriving every summer and it was necessary to have a new clinic near the village, which is where most of them stay, close to the beach. He said it was too big a project for him to take on. He wanted to take life easy after years of working. So I went in front of the medical board that had been appointed to oversee the project. After I was appointed, Fiona became my medical partner in the venture.'

Charlotte was relieved that Iannis was beginning to open up to her. She felt she could ask another question without seeming too presumptuous.

'Where is your wife now?'

'She's back at the hospital in Athens.' He hesitated before taking a deep breath, as if choosing his words carefully. 'Fiona's lover, Lefteris, works there, too. Our divorce has now been finalised so they're planning to marry.'

The flat tone was unnerving. Underneath the calm Charlotte knew that there was a deep turbulence of spirit. Iannis had suffered a great deal. She would love to know the full story of the split.

Neither of them spoke for a short while. Charlotte watched the twilight scene along the waterfront, fascinated by the various activities. Young couples, holding hands, strolled along deep in animated conversation. Older couples walked past with neatly clothed children, some carried by their proud parents, others still in prams or pushchairs. Evening here on Lirakis had a much more relaxed air than the noisy streets of London that she was used to.

'Are you hungry, Charlotte?' Iannis asked suddenly.

'Yes, I—'

'Good, as soon as the sun has set we'll go inside and order some supper. This taverna is always a good place to eat. There's a variety of meat and vegetarian dishes or we can choose between fresh fish, prawns, lobster...do you like seafood?'

'I love it.'

They sat in companiable silence watching the sun disappearing into the sea. For the last few moments the sun hung like a burning crimson sphere over the golden sparkling water before making a final plunge into the depths. Charlotte realised, to her surprise, that she felt completely at ease with Iannis. And she'd only known him for just over a day.

They'd formed a good professional relationship that day. She didn't want anything more. She couldn't help admitting that she found herself deeply attracted to him as a man, but she was holding herself in check. No complications! No emotional hassle! Just a simple...

'OK, let's go inside.'

Iannis was standing up, smiling down at her, one hand outstretched towards her. She took his hand. It seemed such a natural thing to do. He was merely being polite. When he found the table he was looking for beside the open window with a view of the sea, he released her hand and waited for her to sit down.

'Iannis!'

'Stelios!'

Charlotte watched as the two men shook hands, greeting each other with a torrent of rapid Greek.

'Charlotte, this is Stelios who owns the taverna. Stelios, this is the doctor who's come out from England to work at the clinic.'

Stelios smiled at her appraisingly. He was a man of medium stature with a shock of thick white hair. Probably in his fifties, but the gnarled, rugged appearance of his skin made him look older. He'd reached a certain stage in his appearance and would probably look the same for years to come.

'That's good to have someone from England,' Stelios said in a cigarette-scratchy voice.

He paused to catch his breath and coughed heavily for a few seconds.

'In the summer we have all these English people here, and they like to see somebody from their own country. But you must stay on during the winter, Charlotte. That's the best time of the year when it's all quiet and we can sit around and take it easy. Even Iannis can relax in the winter. He paints his boat, he goes fishing. We all do what we want.'

'I'll be back in England in November,' Charlotte said, feeling a sudden sadness descending on her.

She felt homeless at the moment. Her home was supposed to be London but there was absolutely no reason for her to go back. She could already feel that this island had much more to offer her than London. The simple, natural, unhurried life of the people, the warmth of the sun, the sparkling blue sea, the spectacular landscape. She could feel every pore of her being opening up like a flower that had been dried up in a long drought.

'It's a pity you can't stay,' Stelios said.

'Charlotte is on a six-month contract,' Iannis explained quietly.

It was at that moment that Charlotte determined she would enjoy every moment of this six months. In between working with her patients she would get out and about, soak up the sun, swim in the sea, walk over the hills. And in the evenings, if she wasn't working, there would be no harm in letting her hair down.

So long as she didn't become involved! Especially with the gorgeous hunk who'd just invited her to have supper with him. But, on reflection, she was probably safe from involvement with Iannis. From what he'd so far told her about his disastrous marriage, he would be the last man on earth to want a meaningful relationship in the foreseeable future.

Stelios put his hand under Charlotte's elbow in a fatherly way. 'Now, what would you like to eat tonight, my dear? Come into my kitchen and have a look at some of the dishes we've prepared.'

As the three of them threaded their way through the crowded tables, Iannis leaned down and whispered in Charlotte's ear.

'Be careful of Stelios! He may be playing the father figure, but he's terribly fond of the ladies.'

Charlotte looked up at Iannis and was relieved to see the playful grin on his face.

'I can look after myself,' she whispered back.

'Oh, I'm sure of that! Otherwise you wouldn't have come out here all alone without an escort.'

'Huh! Who needs an escort?' she retorted in a bantering tone.

It was fun to feel the light-hearted ambience that had sprung up between them. Charlotte felt a warm glow swimming over her. She'd never totally relaxed with James. Even in the early days, when he'd been hell-bent on conning her into believing all the lies he'd told her.

'So, what are you going to have, Charlotte?'

Iannis's voice cut across her thoughts. He was standing on one side of her, Stelios on the other. Both men were in deep discussion about which of the succulent dishes should be chosen.

'Iannis, it all looks so inviting. I wonder if we could have a small taster of several dishes. I think it's called *mezze* or something like that.'

'An excellent idea!' Iannis said. 'Stelios, just keep the dishes coming and…'

Iannis carried on in Greek, gesticulating towards the various dishes he preferred.

'OK, Charlotte, we can go back to our table.'

It was Iannis's hand under her elbow now, propelling her out of the kitchen back into the crowded dining area of the taverna. A man with an accordian had set himself up on the small raised dais in the corner of the room that served as a stage. A young boy of about five was amusing himself on the drums, banging away to his heart's content.

The youngster was quickly removed by his father as the

real drummer arrived to effect a loud imperious volley of sound that meant everyone had to raise their conversational voices.

A young man stood up and began tuning his violin. Charlotte, who'd learned to play the violin as a child, couldn't imagine how the man could possibly tune up with such a racket going on!

She was laughing as she sank into her seat. 'It's all so warm and friendly in here. Is it always like this?'

Iannis gave her a broad grin. She couldn't help but notice his brilliant white teeth, his chiselled jaw, the way his chin was already shadowed and bristly. He had simply worked all afternoon in Theatre and yet without any thought for his appearance he'd achieved a heart-stopping effect that was to die for!

'Yes, it's always like this,' Iannis said, reaching for the bottle of wine he'd brought with him from the kitchen and filling their glasses. 'Even in the depths of winter. Not so many people as in the summer, of course, but just as lively. You really ought to... No, you've got to get back to London in November, haven't you?'

Not necessarily! Charlotte took a sip of her wine as she reflected that she didn't have to go back to London. She'd resigned from her present hospital position as junior registrar and although her consultant had asked her to return and was holding open an option on her job for next winter there was nothing binding on either side. She looked across the table at Iannis and saw he was watching her, his dark, liquid eyes misty with some emotion she couldn't read.

He leaned across the table. 'I've told you about my disastrous marriage, so now it's your turn to tell me something about yourself. Thirty years old and you've managed to remain single. Quite an achievement!'

His tone was light but she felt she should hold herself in

check. Not give too much away all at once. After all, she'd only known this man since yesterday, even though she felt as if she'd known him a lifetime. It probably helped that they'd both had disastrous relationships and were in the same kind of emotional limbo, feeling shell-shocked and in need of a long period of quiescence.

'I thought I was going to be married,' she began quietly, but realised that she would have to raise her voice if Iannis was to hear her over the noise of the music, laughter and conversations going on around her.

Iannis, sensing her problem, moved his chair closer so that the two of them were sitting side by side at the small table. His arm was pressed against hers. He turned to look at her.

'I'll move back when you've finished your story,' he said, his eyes searching her face as he made it quite clear that it was out of pure necessity that he'd moved closer to her. 'I think it's important I hear what you have to say without the rest of the taverna listening in.'

'Absolutely!' The feel of his arm against hers was unnerving in the most delicious kind of way. She was finding it hard to concentrate. 'Now, where was I?'

She looked out through the window at the twinkling lights of the boats moored against the quayside.

'I think I heard you say that you were going to be married.'

Charlotte nodded. 'That's what I expected was going to happen.'

Absent-mindedly, she picked up her napkin and began creasing and uncreasing it on her lap as memories of her recent stressful situation flooded back.

'But the marriage didn't take place?' Iannis queried gently. 'Why?'

Charlotte gave a harsh laugh. 'My so-called fiancé,

who'd bought me the most expensive diamond ring, was already married.'

'No!'

'Oh, yes.'

Their conversation was interrupted by the arrival of a waiter with a dish of fresh prawns, garnished with slices of lemon, and a Greek salad.

Iannis began shelling one of the prawns on his plate. He lifted it towards Charlotte's mouth. As she took it onto the tip of her tongue she felt a shiver of sensual excitement running through her. Iannis's face was disturbingly close to hers now. The carnival atmosphere continued around them, everyone concerned only with their own little group of friends and relatives. If she and Iannis had been lovers, instead of merely medical colleagues, no one would have noticed if they'd stolen a kiss.

She checked her wicked fantasising as the delicious prawn seemed to melt in her mouth. Quickly she picked up a prawn from her own plate so that Iannis couldn't feed her another one. Why was it that being fed by someone you were attracted to was such a sexy act?

Iannis raised an eyebrow. 'Surely you suspected your fiancé was married?'

Charlotte swallowed the second prawn. 'I should have realised that there was something wrong. With the benefit of hindsight I can see that all the signs were there.'

She sighed. 'I first met James when he turned up one day, quite out of the blue, in Accident and emergency, with an injured wrist. He'd been in a minor collision in central London and had hit his wrist on the steering-wheel, thought it might be broken. It wasn't. He said he lived in France but commuted to London on business every week for a few days. I suppose you could say he chatted me up while I was checking out his wrist.'

'So you arranged to meet?'

'Not immediately, of course. But James could be very charming when he chose to be and he turned on the full charm when he first met me. He came back a few days later. I was surprised to see him because I'd told him he needed no further treatment. He said that now we were no longer in a doctor-patient relationship, would I go out to dinner with him?'

'And that was when it all started?'

Charlotte nodded. 'One thing led to another and we began seeing each other regularly.'

'Is he French?'

'No, James is English. He actually lives in the north of England but I wasn't to know that at the time. He's basically an antique dealer but he dabbles in all sorts of other activities. Always on the lookout for the main chance, I gathered later. Much later, when it was too late!'

She hesitated. Was she boring Iannis with the disastrous account of her affair? No, he looked interested, actually more than interested, as she moved a little closer. The touch of his skin against hers was very soothing.

'I discovered that the ring James gave me was one he'd borrowed from a client who'd asked him to sell it for her. One day, after he'd been with me for the weekend, I couldn't find my ring. I carried on searching for ages but I never found it. James said not to worry, he could easily afford to buy me another one.'

She paused and took a deep breath. 'It was shortly after the ring disappeared that his wife phoned me. Said she'd found my number on James's computer. Were we having an affair or—?'

More dishes were arriving on the table. Charlotte wiped her damp hands on her napkin. It was impossible to talk about the past without feeling upset.

'Everything OK?' The jovial Stelios beamed down at them.

Iannis smiled. 'Excellent!'

He took up a knife and sliced down the back of the superb fish, its scales glistening in the overhead light.

'The poor fish looks as if you're performing a major operation on it,' Charlotte said lightly as she watched Iannis removing a section from the middle and transferring it carefully to her plate.

'At least I don't have to suture this one when we've finished. How does it taste?'

'Mmm, delicious!'

'I think so, too.' He put down the knife. 'I don't want you to lose the thread of your story, Charlotte. Was James's wife angry with you?'

Charlotte glanced around her. Nobody was listening in.

'She wasn't angry with me but she was furious with her husband. She had a strangely laid-back attitude about the whole affair. It had happened before and she was completely philosophical about her terrible marriage. Apparently, I wasn't the first person James had conned. She'd forgiven him several times but this time she said she'd had enough. She even asked me if I still wanted to marry James because if I did she would wish me luck as she was planning to divorce him as soon as she could.'

'I told her it was all a total shock to me to find James was married. I'd known him about a year and for the last few months I'd been having doubts about our relationship but finding out that he was married was the last straw.'

'Was that when you applied for the job out here?'

'No, as it happened, I'd already set the wheels in motion for the job. I'd been feeling dissatisfied with the way things had been going between James and me. There was something not quite right. I couldn't put my finger on it but I felt I had to get away for a while by myself. When the agency phoned me to say I'd got the job I knew I would have to work out what I was going to tell James. Two days later his wife phoned me and saved me agonising over my decision.'

Charlotte was now toying with a stuffed pepper. She put down her fork, realising that she couldn't eat another morsel. There were still small dishes of artichokes cooked in olive oil, stuffed aubergines and fried baby squid virtually untouched.

'Our simple supper has turned into a banquet! Thank you, Iannis.'

He reached over and squeezed her hand. 'Thank you for telling me about yourself. I think I'm beginning to understand why you had to come here. I must admit, I was puzzled why anyone…anyone like you…would want to leave family and friends and come out to a remote island like this.'

Stelios was now putting oranges on the table. 'On the house,' he said, before going back to the kitchen.

Iannis picked up the plate of oranges and held it towards Charlotte. They were still sitting side by side so they could carry on a conversation over the noise, which was growing even louder.

The music was becoming more animated now. People were dancing in the area at the side of the bar, jostling each other, laughing, talking, some of them singing. A couple of small girls—couldn't have been more than two or three, Charlotte thought—who'd been brought along by an elderly lady dressed in black were dancing their little feet off at the side of one of the tables.

'Just look at those little girls, Iannis!' Charlotte laughed, clapping her hands in time to the music as the carnival atmosphere caught up with her. 'Don't they look lovely in those pretty pink dresses?'

Iannis smiled. 'They're twins, as you've probably gathered. I remember delivering them three years ago at their house on the other side of the island. I only just got there in time. Their mother was only sixteen at the time and she was terrified. She hadn't been over to the clinic and had no idea she was expecting two babies. Her mother, grandmother and great-grandmother were doing all they could to calm her.'

'That must have been difficult for you. Were there any complications?'

Iannis gave a wry smile. 'The first baby was OK but the second was a breech. I had to grasp her by the foot and gently ease her out. Fortunately, there were no postnatal complications. The mother has been brilliant with them ever since then. Always bringing the girls into the clinic if she's in doubt about something. The old lady over there is their great-grandmother and she worships the twins. She loves to take them out and show them off to her friends.'

'They're adorable.'

'Yes, they are.' He hesitated. 'Would you like to dance, Charlotte?'

'Oh, I don't know the steps. It's all so different to...'

Iannis was standing up, pushing back his chair, his hand outstretched towards her. 'I can teach you. Anything goes here. Just lose yourself in the music. Go with the flow...'

They moved to the dance floor. Iannis held Charlotte to one side, performing intricate steps that she was having difficulty following. She laughed as Iannis twirled her around a couple of times. Amazingly neither of them trod on each other's toes. She was enjoying this! She realised as she was swept around that some of the dancers had stepped aside to allow them more freedom of movement.

Suddenly she heard delighted cries of *'Ghiatro!'* which she knew meant doctor. The two little girls in pink had run away from their great-grandmother onto the dance floor and were trying to clasp Iannis round the legs.

'Excuse me, Charlotte,' Iannis said as he stopped dancing to pick up the little girls, placing one on each of his shoulders, holding them firmly in place.

They squealed with delight, chattering in rapid Greek to Iannis who was now laughing as he gently turned a few times, executing several careful steps before taking the girls back to their table. They clung to him, but their great-grandmother insisted they must allow the doctor to carry on with his dancing.

Charlotte, meanwhile, had been shown some more steps by an enthusiastic young man who seemed to think she spoke fluent Greek. With a sense of relief she felt Iannis's arm sliding around her waist, directing her expertly into the steps he'd shown her before the small girls had claimed his attention.

There was clapping and cheering from the crowd surrounding them. Charlotte felt as if she'd been transported to a different world. She was certainly going with the flow now, the other revellers around them tapping their feet in time to the music which was becoming more and more lively.

The feel of Iannis's body every time he pulled her against him was sending shivers down her spine. It was such an erotic movement, the muscular vibrations of his body seemed to penetrate her whole being. She could tell the dance was coming to an end because the music was becoming more and more exciting, obviously leading up to a wild climax. There was a long, triumphant roll on the drums and then everyone clapped louder and stamped their feet.

Charlotte knew she would have collapsed against Iannis if he hadn't suddenly swept her into his arms, twirling her round with her feet off the ground.

For a few seconds time seemed to stand still. The cheers, laughter and clapping continued around them, but for Charlotte this was a unique moment. It was as if the two of them had been cast away on an island remote from everyone. She was trying to catch her breath as she looked up at Iannis. He, too, was breathing deeply, his eyes holding a bright, excited expression.

He put his hand on the small of her back, gently guiding her through the crush of people at the side of the dance floor.

'Let's sit outside,' he said.

The air was welcomingly cooler when they emerged from the crowded taverna to find a table near the water. As Charlotte sat down again, she knew that she would always remember that moment out there on the dance floor. The moment when she'd felt as if she'd met a soul mate. Someone she was attracted to much more than she wanted to be. Someone who might cause so many emotional complications that she wasn't ready to face yet.

She looked up at the night sky, marvelling at the tiny, twinkling points of light hanging over the little island like a canopy of diamonds. The moon was illuminating a nearby cloud, giving it a liquid glow around its ragged, candy-floss edges. As she watched, mesmerised by all this natural beauty, a shooting star suddenly shot across the sky before falling towards the earth and disappearing. She simply had to make a wish, even though she didn't believe in such superstitious nonsense any more. Or did she…?

As she closed her eyes the haunting melody of a song ran through her brain. Wish on a star… She was wishing…

She opened her eyes and saw that Iannis was watching her.

He smiled, the sort of heartrending smile that Charlotte could do without at this sensitive time when she was trying to keep control of her runaway emotions.

'You made a wish, didn't you?' he said quietly.

'Maybe. Did you?'

'Doesn't everyone?' he said huskily. 'That's what makes the world go round. The magic of playing games we don't believe in any more. Strange rituals we learned as a child and still keep going.'

She nodded. 'Yes. Why do we do it?'

'I don't know. It's some primaeval force deep down inside us, like the feelings we can't control, I suppose…' His voice trailed away.

Charlotte remained quiet, sensing that if she said anything more she would be getting herself into deep water. She didn't know where this conversation was heading. Any moment now they might touch on romance and that was something she wanted to avoid. She liked the idea of Iannis being a soul mate but she didn't want to spoil this by introducing dangerous elements at this early stage in their fragile relationship.

Iannis clasped his hands beneath the table as he listened to Charlotte. She looked so beautiful bathed in moonlight. It hadn't been easy this evening to convince himself that he mustn't show Charlotte that he found her extremely attractive.

He'd asked her to dance so that he could be near her. So that he would have a legitimate excuse for holding her in his arms. And he'd given in to sheer joyful exuberance at the end of the dance when he'd lifted her off her feet and twirled her around. As light as a feather she'd been, and the feel of her soft curving body against his had been sheer agony. Delicious agony, though! He wouldn't have missed a moment of it but…

His mobile was ringing. *'Ne?'*

Charlotte had found it strange at first that the Greek for 'yes' was *'ne'*. It sounded so negative. Iannis was smiling now, so it couldn't be an emergency. Probably just a social call, one of his admirers inviting him for a drink perhaps. She was surprised at the way she was hoping Iannis wouldn't leave her at this point in the evening when she was feeling so happy, so mellow, so…so relaxed and longing to embrace her new life and all the experiences that were coming her way.

'That was the hospital. The night nurse says that little Vasilis wants to see me before he goes to sleep.'

'Any particular reason?'

Iannis grinned. 'Vasilis wants to say goodnight to me.'

Charlotte smiled. 'That's nice.'

'I was going to go back anyway. But apparently he's trying to stay awake till I arrive. Oh, and he said he'd like to see that nice lady doctor as well.'

Charlotte pushed back her chair, glad that she had been included. She didn't want the evening to end here, even though it would be much safer if it did.

Vasilis was propped back against his pillows. He gave them a tight little smile when they went into the room. His mother got up from her chair and said she would go for her supper while the doctors were with Vasilis.

Iannis checked under the edge of the dressing that stretched across the little boy's throat. No further bleeding. The wound looked healthy.

Charlotte and Iannis chatted quietly to their little patient.

Vasilis asked, sleepily, if they would tell him a story. Iannis agreed and began an exciting tale about one of the Greek gods. Charlotte found she could understand most of the Greek words because she'd heard the story as a child. She wondered momentarily if it was going to be too stimulating for a bedtime story but she needn't have worried. Five minutes into the story Vasilis had fallen fast asleep. They waited quietly until his mother returned before leaving.

Tatiana was profuse in her thanks as they were leaving. Said she didn't know what she would have done if they hadn't saved her son. She would be eternally grateful to them both.

'Nice to be appreciated like that,' Charlotte said as they walked away down the corridor together. 'We're only doing our job, after all.'

'It happens out here all the time,' Iannis said. 'The islanders are a close community and I think that helps to bind us together.'

'I've enjoyed meeting people today,' Charlotte said quietly. 'They're all so friendly and helpful.'

Iannis stopped outside the door of his office and turned to face her. 'So you think you're going to be happy out here?'

'Oh, yes!' She tried to check some of her enthusiasm, knowing it was safer to stay cool.

She turned away. How could she stay cool after the wonderful evening they'd spent together?

'Charlotte?'

'Yes?'

She turned back, trying to compose her features so Iannis wouldn't know she wanted more from him. Surely he was going to ask her in for a nightcap or something? She knew how to keep her emotions under control in such a situation.

'How do you find your room?'

'Well, it's not difficult, it's just in the next section of the building. I thought…'

Iannis was smiling. 'Yes, I know where it is. My own room is in the same section. What I meant was, is everything OK for you there?'

'Oh, yes, of course.'

Iannis remained still, looking down at her with an enigmatic expression. She knew with a sinking feeling that this was the end of the evening.

'If there's anything you're missing from your room, you only have to ask my secretary and—'

'It's fine!' She turned away. 'Can't wait to get back to it. It's been a long day. Goodnight, Iannis. *Kali nichte.*'

'Charlotte…'

'Yes?' She turned back, her heart throbbing with anticipation.

'Thank you for this evening.' He leaned forward and kissed her cheek.

The touch of his lips unnerved her. But it was a fleeting kiss, over before it had really begun. The sort of kiss she'd often experienced from a friendly acquaintance. She'd wanted so much more, but perversely she was glad that Iannis had kept the mood light at the end of their evening together.

She turned away and moved off down the corridor. As she turned the corner she looked back but Iannis had already gone into his office. She could picture him settling down to some paperwork. Not giving her a second thought. Whereas she knew she would find it very difficult to sleep tonight after she'd experienced such a maelstrom of conflicting emotions.

Iannis closed the door behind him and leaned against it, breathing deeply. He'd come so close to inviting Charlotte back to his room. It had been so difficult, watching her walk away from him towards the medical residents' quarters and remaining behind pretending he had work to do. Well, he did have work to do but nothing that couldn't wait until morning.

He strode across to the desk and sat down, leaning forward to put both elbows on the desk and supporting his head in his hands. Charlotte had been frank with him this evening. She'd told him about her disastrous love life. She was obviously furious that she'd been deceived. But was she broken-hearted? Was she so wounded that she would have difficulty forming another relationship?

He lifted his head and leaned back in his chair. He would have to tread carefully with Charlotte if he wanted to have any kind of relationship with her. She was so different to the other women he'd gone out with since Fiona had left him. Until this evening he'd gone through the motions when he'd taken someone out. They had been interesting diversions, but they hadn't meant anything or affected him emotionally.

But Charlotte was different. She was the sort of girl he wanted to spend more time with. Tonight, as he'd held her in his arms on the dance floor, he'd wanted to carry her away, out of the taverna and find some romantic spot where he could make love to her…

He groaned as he felt the pain of his unconsummated passion deep down in his body. He'd only known Charlotte one day and she was already turning his world upside down. He thought he'd got his life sorted, thought he would never feel like this again. He hadn't wanted this to happen so soon. He'd resisted the temptation tonight but there would be other nights when he knew he might find it impossible to ignore his strong feelings…

CHAPTER FOUR

'WOULD you like to come over to see Sophia with me when you've finished, Charlotte?' Iannis asked.

Charlotte looked up from the case notes she was entering into the computer.

'That's my last patient for this morning so, yes, I'd like to see how Sophia is getting on. I've also promised to look in on Richard Horton this morning in the health and fitness section. He's not too happy with the health programme the staff have drawn up for him.'

Iannis pulled a wry face. 'You could be there all day with Richard. He seems to have...what's that strange English phrase? He's taken a shine to you, Charlotte.'

Charlotte smiled. 'Iannis, he's a lonely, disheartened patient. Since the operation on his knee he's taken the big decision to sell his company, invest the proceeds and leave the rat race so—'

'Rat race?'

'Silly expression for all that's wrong about working under pressure too much.'

'Well, Richard may have given up on working for a living but he's certainly working on getting fit,' Iannis said. 'Don't let him overdo the exercises on the knee. And don't let him keep you too long, will you?'

'I'll be at my most professional and escape as soon as I can.'

'I'll pick you up from there in half an hour. OK?'

'Fine!'

As Iannis went back to his office, Charlotte turned back

to the screen to check what she'd written. There had been a quick succession of tourist patients arriving this morning, most of them with minor complaints. One young woman, who'd cut herself badly with a tin opener, had required a couple of stitches and a great deal of reassurance to stem the flow of her tears. An overweight, middle-aged man had suffered chest pains after jogging early in the morning. He had been convinced he'd been having a heart attack. After a full examination, Charlotte had been able to reassure him that his heart was sound.

The causes of the problem had probably been the greasy fried breakfast he'd treated himself to before setting out, the fact that he hadn't jogged for about ten years and was grossly overweight. Charlotte had given the man a diet sheet and advised that he should take regular but gentle exercise to begin with.

She looked out of the window. Through the trees she could see some of the holiday apartments by the sea in the nearby bay. They were filling up fast and it was only June. She was beginning to realise just how stretched their medical resources would be during July and August.

Charlotte switched off her computer and leaned back in her chair. She'd been here almost a month now, a month in which she'd experienced some pretty disturbing emotional turmoil deep down inside herself. The problem was that she was never able to relax completely when she was with Iannis. She found him far too attractive. And she knew that if he indicated that he felt the same way about her she would be hopelessly sunk!

Fortunately, Iannis always seemed to play it cool. He often suggested a drink at the taverna after work. Sometimes the two of them would stay on for supper, but at the end of the evening they went their separate ways.

She knew that was the safest way for the evenings to end, but it was also the most frustrating!

Iannis's room was a few feet down the corridor from hers. Sometimes in the night she would lie awake thinking about him, wondering how much longer she could go on pretending that this basically platonic friendship was all she wanted. Was it self-restraint that Iannis was showing or did he simply not fancy her?

She'd tried to convince herself that either way it was much better that they should remain just good friends, but the perverse side of her still wanted more, even though she knew, from past experience, that it might be an emotional disaster.

There was a knock on her door before it was tentatively pushed open. A small boy peeped in.

'Vasilis! Come in, come in. What a lovely surprise!'

'Iannis is going to check on my neck but I asked if I could come and see you first, Charlotte. My mother is talking to Iannis.'

The little boy smiled as Charlotte came round the desk and knelt down so that his eyes were level with her own. He held out his arms towards her and she gave him a hug before making a quick appraisal of the long scar on Vasilis's neck. She remembered the day he'd come in, covered in blood, with his weeping mother, frightened out of her mind. Four weeks on, the scar looked clean and healthy but very visible. It would fade with time but never disappear totally.

'Everybody at school thinks my scar is amazing,' Vasilis said, his eyes dancing with mischief. 'I told one boy I'd been bitten by a shark and he thought that was really cool. Another boy thinks I was mauled by a wild dog.'

Charlotte smiled. 'Vasilis, you're wicked! I bet all your friends think you were very brave.'

Vasilis nodded happily. 'One of my friends painted a scar on his neck, said he'd been half eaten by a lion, but we all knew it wasn't real because there aren't any lions on Lirakis, are there? I'd better go back to Iannis now. I promised not to stay long.'

Charlotte stood up. 'And I've got to go off and see another patient.' She took hold of Vasilis's hand and walked with him to Iannis's office, taking him inside so that she could have a few words with his mother.

Iannis glanced at his watch pointedly.

Charlotte nodded. 'It's OK, Iannis, I'm on my way right now. Bye, everybody.'

She walked out of the clinic and took the path that led through the trees to the health and fitness section.

Her patient would be waiting for her. Richard Horton could be very demanding. Remembering how he'd threatened to sue them after he'd fallen off the treadmill, she was glad she'd never been one of his employees when he'd been a company director. Richard had a lot of anger and frustration inside him.

Charlotte was a little apprehensive about his decision to opt out of the rat race and choose a healthier lifestyle. It wasn't just a whim that he was indulging in for a short time. Every time she went to see him she realised that he was determined to make a go of it. Apparently, after his summer here on Lirakis he was going to take things much easier. She only hoped that he wouldn't waver in his decision when he had to lead a less luxurious lifestyle.

She found her patient in the yoga class outside under the trees. He appeared to be meditating but as she approached he got up from the sparse, dried grass and moved away from the group.

'Thank you for coming, Charlotte,' Richard said briskly, running a hand through his grey-streaked hair. 'I know you must have a busy schedule so I do appreciate you taking the time.'

Richard was a tall, powerfully built man in his fifties. When Charlotte had first met him she'd found him intimidating but she'd soon realised that he was a lost soul, searching to find some meaning to his life. He'd told her his wife had recently left him, taking the children with her because he'd forgotten to turn up for the children's sports day.

'Can you imagine, Charlotte? I was working flat out to earn enough to give my wife and children a fantastic lifestyle,' he'd told her. 'And she left me because my secretary had forgotten to remind me about sports day!'

But Charlotte had realised there had been more to it than that. There were always two sides to every story. Just as James's wife had reached the end of her tether, so Richard's wife must have had an awful lot to put up with.

'I haven't got very much time, Richard,' Charlotte said as she walked beside her patient, 'so perhaps you'd like to sit out here and tell me your problems. On the seat under that tree would be a good place.'

'It's about my knee,' Richard said, as they settled under the welcome shade of the tall scented pine tree. 'That surgeon friend of Iannis's in Athens did a good job on it. I'm sure I could do more exercise by now. I want to be a hundred per cent fit next month when my children come out.'

'I didn't know your children were coming out to Lirakis. That will be nice for you. But, Richard, you mustn't try to rush your convalescence. Please, be guided by what the physiotherapist says. She knows exactly how much you can do with that knee.'

Richard frowned. 'But it's taking much longer than I thought it would.'

'It will take time, Richard.' Charlotte looked down at her

patient's knee beneath the expensive designer shorts. The tiny scar from the keyhole surgery was still visible, otherwise it looked completely normal.

'Would you like to show me how you can extend your knee horizontally? Gently, gently...'

Richard stretched his leg, glancing sideways at Charlotte to see if she was impressed.

'You're making excellent progress. Don't try to rush your treatment. You've told me you've decided to stay for the summer. When you go back to England you'll be fighting fit.'

'I'm not sure if I'll ever want to go back to the UK,' Richard said quietly.

'I know the feeling,' Charlotte said gently.

'Do you?' Richard looked surprised. 'It's this peaceful island. It sort of wraps itself around you, doesn't it, Charlotte?'

She swallowed hard. 'Certainly does. It's having a profound effect on me and I've seen a great change in you, Richard.'

'Have you? A change for the better?'

Charlotte hesitated. 'Well, you were very tense when you first arrived. Now...'

She broke off as she saw Iannis's black Jeep coming down the track that led through a gap in the trees.

'I'll have to go, Richard. Iannis and I have to go over to the other side of the island to see a patient.'

'Will you come back tomorrow?'

'I'll try to fit you in at the end of the morning clinic. But we're getting to the height of the tourist season and it's not always possible. If there's an emergency then of course...'

Iannis hooted impatiently.

'Goodbye, Richard. Take care. I'll come again soon.'

* * *

'So how's our meniscectomy patient today?' Iannis asked, as he helped Charlotte climb up into the Jeep.

'Physically he's fine,' Charlotte said as she strapped herself into her seat. 'But emotionally, I'm not sure.'

'Richard's certainly got problems,' Iannis said as he steered the vehicle round the trees and headed off towards the road over the hill. 'I think he's still in love with his wife and she's refusing to take him back.'

'That must be a very sad situation for him,' Charlotte said. 'At least I'd got over my infatuation with James by the time I heard that he was already married. I mean...'

Iannis glanced sideways momentarily at the firm set of Charlotte's jaw. He felt a definite lifting of his spirits. For the whole of the time he'd known Charlotte, all four weeks of it, he'd imagined she might be pining for her ex-lover. He'd deliberately soft-pedalled his emotions, held back from making advances, gone back to his room in a state of furious frustration so many times. But if he'd known she'd recovered from her disastrous affair...

'I mean, you've got to move on, haven't you, Iannis? But it must be so awful if you're still in love.' She hesitated. 'How about your situation with your ex-wife? Are you still in love with her or...?' She broke off, sensing that she'd gone too far. 'I'm sorry Iannis, that was a much too personal question. Forget I asked it.'

'That's OK.' Iannis was silent as he steered the Jeep round a hairpin bend. They soon reached the top of the hill and began cruising down the other side.

Charlotte looked down at the greeny blue spread of the bay. A tiny fishing boat was moored near its entrance. Gulls swooped down near it, alighting on the deck, waiting hungrily for a share in the catch. She sensed that Iannis, beside her, was tense. He was breathing deeply, heavily, like a man under some strain.

Iannis gripped the wheel as he drove down towards the sea. Charlotte's question about whether he was still in love with Fiona had taken him by surprise. It wasn't the sort of thing he'd ever asked himself. He had a dull ache in the pit of his stomach whenever he thought about his failed marriage, but that was because he was mourning for the marriage that hadn't turned out as he'd intended. The marriage that never was.

'I loved Fiona,' he said quietly. 'But not any more.'

Charlotte felt a lifting of her spirits. She'd thought he was still carrying a torch for his ex-wife. It was good to know she didn't have a rival! But she realised that the main problem after being in a relationship where trust has been broken was learning to trust again. She was unsure if she could do that herself. A deep meaningful, trusting relationship was still out of the question, but a short, no-strings-attached affair could be just the answer.

Glancing at Iannis's rugged profile, she felt a heightening of her emotions, a longing to be held in his arms. It wasn't just sexual frustration. It was something more than that. She wondered if perhaps Iannis was waiting for her to make the first move. In that case...

Iannis brought the Jeep to a halt at the start of the sandy path that led to Sophia's house. Charlotte climbed down, revelling in the feel of Iannis's strong arms as he helped her.

Iannis released his grip on her waist and strode ahead.

The waves at the side of the path were breaking gently on the shore. The sky above mirrored the blue sheen of the sea. Charlotte took in a deep breath of the salt-scented air. What a place to work! It wasn't like work as she'd always known it. And she'd never found herself working with such an interesting colleague before. Interesting was too mild a word to express what she felt about Iannis but for the moment that was all she was going to allow herself.

Sophia and Karlos were sitting outside on the terrace.

'Not bad news, I hope?' Sophia said, walking across to meet them.

'What do you mean?' Iannis asked.

'Well, I know you told me the tests on my blood had detected no abnormality but I wondered if something else had been discovered.'

Iannis put an arm around Sophia's thickening waist and escorted her back to her seat on the terrace. 'Sophia, your tests were very encouraging and so no further tests will be made.'

'But you said that the tests weren't conclusive,' Sophia said.

'I said that the blood serum screening was able to detect two out of three cases of Down's syndrome and four out of five spina bifida cases. Your tests didn't reveal any abnormality so that's why I'm saying the results are very encouraging. Not totally conclusive but on the present findings we're hoping for a completely normal baby. If you wanted to be one hundred per cent sure then we would have done an amniocentesis.'

'Sophia, you've had this explained so many times, darling,' Karlos said, squeezing his wife's hand.

He looked across the table at the two doctors. 'You've been really great with Sophia. She hasn't worried at all since we got the results of the test. It was just seeing you coming along the path that made her wonder if there was something wrong.'

Iannis gave a wry smile. 'I understand. Look, why don't you bring Sophia over to see me at the clinic, Karlos?'

'I hate hospitals!' Sophia said.

'The clinic isn't a hospital,' Charlotte said. 'It's really friendly. We need to see you regularly during your pregnancy, Sophia. And if you don't come to us, we'll have to come to see you.'

Sophia smiled broadly. 'I like you to visit me as my friends but not when you want to start poking around to see what's happening to the baby. You don't want to examine me today, do you?'

'Not if you don't want me to,' Iannis said quietly. 'But I'd like to see you at the clinic during the next couple of weeks so that we can give you an ultrasound. How have you been feeling since we last saw you?'

'Fine! And I've stopped feeling sick in the mornings.'

'Still taking the tablets I gave you?' Charlotte asked.

'When she remembers!' Karlos said, looking fondly at his wife with the sort of expression parents reserved for naughty children.

Sophia grinned. 'My mother never took any tablets and look at me!'

'Exactly!' Karlos said.

Sophia picked up a cushion and aimed it at her husband's head.

Karlos caught it and placed it on the chair beside him before standing up. 'What can I get you folks to drink?'

'We can't stay,' Iannis said, rising to his feet. 'Duty calls. We wanted to make sure that Sophia would keep up her appointments.'

'Don't worry, Iannis,' Karlos said, as he walked beside them to the start of the path. 'I'll see that Sophia toes the line from now on. We both want this baby to be as healthy as possible.'

* * *

'This isn't the way back to the clinic,' Charlotte said as Iannis steered the Jeep off the main track at the top of the hill.

'I thought we could have our lunch-break in more pleasing surroundings.'

Iannis was concentrating on the bumpy track ahead of him. The sandy surface was pitted roughly with large stones. They were driving down now towards another bay.

'It looks completely deserted down there. Is there a taverna?'

Iannis smiled. 'There's absolutely nothing there except sea and sand. I've thrown some provisions into the back of the Jeep so we can have a picnic.'

She settled back against her seat. 'That's nice.'

'I'm glad you approve. I haven't brought any plates or anything.'

She smiled. 'Why would we need plates in a natural environment like this?'

'Exactly!'

Charlotte raised one eyebrow. 'So this is the duty you told Karlos was calling us, is it?'

Iannis laughed. 'Yes, I thought it was time I showed you something of the island.'

'So I'm a duty, am I?'

'You're an important member of my staff. Apart from that, a long lunch-break is part of the perks of working at the clinic. We have to work whenever the patients need us so we take time off when we can get it. Hold tight, here we go...!'

The vehicle was skidding on the sand. Iannis turned the steering wheel into the skid and brought the vehicle to a halt, leaning over the edge of the hillside.

'Phew! That was a near thing!' Iannis turned to look at Charlotte. 'Are you OK?'

'Never better. I like a bit of excitement in the middle of the day. It doesn't look as if this track is used very often.'

Iannis reached for a tissue from the glove compartment and wiped the beads of sweat from his forehead.

'Very few people come down here. It's one of the deserted beaches, so much more fun than the tourist beaches. When I want to relax I escape down here, bring some bread and cheese, swim, fall asleep...'

'Answer your mobile and go rushing back to the clinic.'

Iannis laughed. 'You've got it! I think we'd better walk from here. That storm we had last night has created far too many ruts in the track. If the Jeep packs in down here, we'll have to walk back to the clinic.'

'Are we expecting any patients this afternoon?' Charlotte asked as she waited at the rear of the vehicle to be given some provisions to carry.

'There are no appointments. Our official opening time is mornings only. Yes, don't laugh. I know it doesn't work that way. That is what the tourists are told when they first arrive. But they know they'll be seen any time, day or night, if it's an emergency.'

'It must be difficult during the height of summer.' Charlotte shouldered the small bag Iannis handed over to her.

'It is, but the off-season makes up for it.'

'So I'm told...but I won't be here then.'

'You'll be back in London, going to theatres, cinemas and—'

'Trekking through the dark, wet streets, enveloped in thick woollies, cloaked in waterproofs.'

Iannis lifted a large rucksack onto his back. 'Sounds fun!'

Charlotte smiled as she began to follow Iannis down a twisty path that went down the hillside to the beach.

'I'd rather be here,' she said softly, as she breathed in the scent of the herbs on the hillside. 'Mmm, that's oregano, isn't it?'

She held a green stem in her hand, rubbing the scented fronds between her thumb and forefinger.

Iannis turned. 'Yes, that's oregano.'

'I've never seen it growing in its natural state. You can buy it in the supermarket but it won't taste as good as this.'

For a few moments Iannis watched her as she held the fragrant herb to her nose. He felt a pang of apprehension running through him. Charlotte looked so young, so innocent. Difficult to believe she'd been battle-scarred by a disastrous relationship. She looked like a young girl out on her first date.

He checked himself. This wasn't a date. This was simply a friendly picnic with a colleague. Over the last four weeks he'd tried very hard to maintain a friendly relationship. He didn't want to reveal how much he longed for more. He'd made this picnic sound as if he'd only just thought up the idea today. But he'd agonised over it for days. Wondered if he dared trust himself not to spoil a simple, innocent friendship that was going so well. Charlotte was an excellent doctor. She'd made such a difference to his life at the clinic. He needed her as a professional. Why didn't he simply try harder to keep his emotions under control?

He knew he couldn't cope with the emotional complications of an affair. He didn't love Fiona any more but the harm she'd done by her duplicity still haunted him. He was convinced he could never go through the agony of being emotionally traumatised again. Was that how Charlotte was feeling? And if he did show that he was attracted to her, would their warm, easygoing, friendly relationship be shattered, never to be revived?

He continued to walk down the steep path. Behind him

he could hear Charlotte's steady breathing and knew that she was keeping up with his fast pace. He was longing to reach the shore, longing yet apprehensive. Once they were alone together with only the birds to watch them…that was when he would have to hold onto his feelings. He mustn't allow himself to spoil what they had now. Charlotte was like a fragile flower. If he was too rough with her…

'Oh, it's so beautiful!' Charlotte cried out as they reached the shore.

She was already removing her rucksack, taking off her sandals and heading for the sea. Iannis followed suit and caught up with her at the edge of the sand.

She turned to look at him. 'Iannis, I wish you'd told me we were coming to a lovely beach like this. I'd love to swim but…'

She stared at Iannis, her green eyes beguiling and innocent.

Iannis looked down at her, a rakish grin on his face. 'So there's nobody to see you except me and I'm a doctor, or hadn't you noticed? When you've seen one naked body, you've seen them all.'

'OK,' Charlotte said glibly, as she peeled off her clothes and ran quickly into the waves.

Iannis was slightly slower. He told himself that it wasn't simply that he wanted to witness the sight of Charlotte's lovely body disappearing beneath the water. He wanted to make sure that their clothes would be above the tide line and wouldn't float out on the next wave. That was the only reason he was now standing there, shielding his eyes as he watched Charlotte striking out to sea.

'Don't go too far out!' he called. 'There are some treacherous currents beyond those rocks.'

'I'm not going that far,' she called, turning onto her back and looking up at the sky.

She closed her eyes as she lay back in the water, revelling in the cool feeling of being enveloped in a kind of healing balm. Yes, she knew that the sea did have special healing properties and it was certainly working its magic on her now. Turning over, she saw that Iannis was swimming close by. The natural state of their bodies was of no concern to her. It was as if they'd known each other for years.

With the added interest that they had yet to get to know each other more intimately. She shivered at the exciting prospect. Would it ever happen? Would Iannis assume that she was lying here flaunting her body on the surface of the water so that he would want to make love to her?

'You're shivering. Are you cold, Charlotte?'

She trod water. 'No, I think it's simply the contrast between the heat of the land and the coolness of the sea. Oh, look, Iannis, is that a dolphin out there?'

She shaded her eyes as she stared out beyond the rocks.

'Certainly is! And it's brought some friends along.'

'Wow! What a display they're putting on! It's almost as if they know we're watching and they're showing off.'

She continued to stare across the water, utterly fascinated as several dolphins leapt out of the sea in quick succession, forming arcs above the sea with their gleaming black bodies and curved heads.

'They do know we're watching and, yes, I think they're putting on the display just for the two of us, Charlotte.'

'Let's get closer. With any luck we might be able to swim with them… Oh, they're swimming away.'

Iannis laughed and then spluttered as he swallowed some sea water. 'I think they heard you. That's why they're heading off.'

Charlotte turned back towards Iannis who was almost touching her now.

'Perhaps they're shy. Oh, but they were so spectacular. I only wanted to swim near them, perhaps lean over and stroke one of them, Iannis.'

'Well, you'll have to make do with me,' he said, his voice croaky with the effect of the sea water he'd just swallowed by mistake.

'Ah, you poor thing,' Charlotte said, reaching out to touch Iannis's cheek. 'You're gasping for breath.'

'I think I need the kiss of life,' Iannis said huskily, placing one arm around Charlotte's shoulders and drawing her into his embrace.

Her feet were desperately treading water as she felt Iannis's lips on hers. Their first real kiss on the lips. She felt her treacherous naked body flaming with reaction. The deep water out here was cool but she was on fire as she returned his kiss, closing her eyes in delicious anticipation of more…

Iannis's hands were caressing her naked body. Within moments, his sensual caresses were driving her wild with desire. Was it possible to make love out here in this deep water? Or would they both become oblivious to where they were and begin sinking into the depths…?

Charlotte pulled herself away, gasping for breath. Iannis's eyes, close to hers, held a tender expression.

'We should be heading back,' she said quickly.

'Thank you for the kiss of life,' he said softly, running his hand over her back with tantalising promise. 'I'm feeling much stronger now. If you're tired I can take you back to shore using the lifesaving position.'

'Which one?' she asked, striking out for the shore, trying to shake off the tremors of sensual excitement that were running through her body.

'The most usual one is where I hold you on my chest, swim with my legs and—'

'You'd have to knock me out first,' she called gaily.

'Only if you struggled!'

'Oh, I wouldn't struggle.'

I'd be a pushover, she thought as she increased her pace. What on earth was she doing, swimming naked in the sea, flirting madly with the most drop-dead gorgeous hunk of a man she fancied rotten? This wasn't what she'd intended would happen when she'd left London. It certainly wasn't…but it was such fun! Whatever happened today—and she couldn't help hoping that the mood wouldn't change when they reached dry land—she wouldn't put a stop to it. A relationship that made her feel this good should be allowed to continue…and progress! It would be such a waste to try to call a halt now…

Reaching the shore, she ran along at the edge of the water, holding her salty face up to the sun. Iannis fell into step beside her.

'Natural drying!' she called between breaths. 'Who needs a towel when the sun is this hot?'

'We'd better slap on some skin protection,' Iannis said. 'I've got a bottle in with the picnic things. I packed it next to the vinaigrette.' He grinned. 'We'd better not get the bottles muddled up.'

Charlotte laughed. 'Let's go and get started.'

She retraced her steps to reach her pile of clothes. Quickly, she pulled on her briefs and skirt, knotting her white shirt around her waist. Iannis was wearing his lightweight chinos, his shirt draped across his back, tied loosely around his neck.

He stood looking down on her. 'It's too hot for clothes.'

'I agree, but they're practical to wear while we have our picnic. Think of all that sand scratching everywhere.'

Iannis laughed. 'I'm fully prepared. I've brought a sheet to spread over the sand.'

They went back to the edge of the beach where they'd left their rucksacks. Charlotte began unpacking the food while Iannis uncorked a bottle of retsina. He poured a glass for Charlotte and held it out to her across the stretch of white cotton which doubled as a tablecloth-cum-seating area.

'*Sigiya!* Good health!' He raised his glass to hers.

The both smiled when the unbreakable Perspex glasses made a dull thud instead of a clinking sound. Charlotte scooped out a small hollow in the sand in which to prop up her glass while she continued to help with preparing the picnic.

'Iannis, this is a real feast! How many guests were you planning to invite?'

Iannis hunkered back on his heels and grinned at her. 'I hadn't decided when I set off this morning. It was a spur-of-the-moment thing. Lovely day, lovely girl in my car…that sort of thing…'

He was trying hard to keep the atmosphere light. He knew he'd got carried away in the water but who could blame him when Charlotte's lovely naked body had been so close to his? She'd seemed to respond to his advances…well, she hadn't pushed him away!

'Have some taramasalata, Charlotte.' He passed the carton across the cloth towards her.

Charlotte broke off a piece of crusty bread and ate it with some of the tangy fish roe pâté. Next she had some feta cheese and olives before trying one of the small, flaky-pastry spinach pies.

'What are these called, Iannis?'

'Spanokopita. They were delivered fresh this morning from the bakery in the town.'

'They're delicious!'

Iannis reached across and topped up her glass in its specially made sandy holder.

She took a sip, replaced her glass and reached for a fresh apricot. It was perfectly ripe and soft to the touch. She lay back, her elbows in the sand, looking up at the rays of the sun that filtered through the shady fir tree. The sound of the waves lapping on the shore, the occasional tinkling of a goat's bell on the hill, the cry of the gulls were the only sounds. It was like being marooned on their very own desert island.

'This is all so beautiful,' she said softly, almost to herself.

Iannis moved across and stretched out beside her. 'I'm glad madam approves of my choice of restaurant.'

He told himself that he was sticking to his rules. Keeping a light atmosphere. Wanting nothing more than…

He raised himself on one elbow and looked down at Charlotte. Her lips were parted expectantly. He remembered the feel of her soft lips as they'd kissed in the water. She hadn't resisted. If she resisted now he would…

Charlotte felt a sensual tremor of excitement as Iannis lowered his head towards hers. She revelled in the wild anticipation that flooded through her and when he kissed her she closed her eyes and raised her arms to hold him against her. They were safe on dry land now. She didn't have to worry about drowning…only about drowning herself in this hard, virile man.

She could feel the hardness of his passion mounting as she clung to him. There was no turning back now. No pretending that she didn't feel deeply about him. His caressing hands were too stimulating, too erotic, more than she could bear… If he were to hold back now…leaving her high and dry, longing to feel the thrust of him inside her and…

'Ah-h!' She heard the loud ecstatic moan as if it came

from somewhere above her before she realised it was her own voice. She was no longer in control. She'd given herself up completely. As Iannis entered her the tension increased.

Yes, oh, yes, she'd never felt like this before…

She cried out as she climaxed in a rush of ethereal release. Over and over she cried out until, completely spent and satiated, she relaxed, limp and exhausted, against Iannis's hard, muscular body.

He pulled her into his arms again, but this time with a gentleness that brought tears to her eyes. Whatever the outcome of this act of love, she would always remember her first time with Iannis.

With her head cradled on his chest she fell into a dreamless sleep.

Charlotte was disturbed by a tinkling sound and her first thought was that it was a goat's bell. She kept her eyes closed, not wanting to come back to earth again. Something was tickling her nose. She opened her eyes. Iannis was teasing her with a small fir branch.

She smiled up at him, stretching her legs out, enjoying the relaxed feeling of her sexually satisfied body. The fact that she was naked again didn't matter any more. The time for reckoning would come later but for the moment she was still living on her make-believe desert island.

'I've just had a call on my mobile from the clinic. We'll have to go back.'

'Oh, no!'

'Oh, yes!' He was smiling down at her with infinite tenderness. 'You can stay here if you like, Charlotte, but you'll have a long way to walk back.'

'I'll get dressed.'

Suddenly she felt shy again. It was as if they'd had a

brief interlude on another planet. None of this was part of the real world. They had to get back to reality, and quickly.

Iannis reached towards her, his fingers caressing her cheek. 'Before we go I want to say that—'

'Don't, Iannis. Don't say anything. It happened. Let's not try to work out why or we might spoil it.'

'But it was wonderful for me and…' His voice trailed away. He knew Charlotte didn't want to hear any more. She was right. Analysing what had happened between them would only spoil it.

'And it was wonderful for me,' she said softly as she realised that their relationship had inevitably changed. They couldn't go back now…even if they wanted to.

CHAPTER FIVE

IANNIS put one arm on the back of Charlotte's seat as he turned to look out of the back window of the Jeep, cautiously reversing up the rutted, sandy track.

'There's a turning point higher up the hill,' he explained, when Charlotte suggested he attempt to turn round from where they were parked. 'If I try to turn here we'll only get stuck in the sand and probably have to stay here all night.'

'A night on a bare mountain. It's a piece of music I've heard somewhere,' she added quickly.

Iannis smiled. 'I thought you were propositioning me.'

'As if I would! Anyway, what's the problem back at the clinic?'

They'd reached the turning point in the track. Iannis swung the wheel a couple of times and they were going forward again.

Iannis frowned. 'I'm not sure. Marina simply said it wasn't an emergency but there was someone insisting they had to see me. She claimed she couldn't hear what I was saying when I started asking questions. Apparently, my reply was very faint so she would explain when I got back.'

'Seems very strange.'

'Yes, it does. Marina is usually brilliant at fending off unwanted visitors but this time it must be a very insistent person. And I wouldn't want Marina to be upset by whoever it is. She's worth her weight in gold. The office work would grind to a halt if she decided to leave. I'm notoriously bad at keeping up with my paperwork. If Marina hadn't prodded me into replying to Fiona's solicitor the divorce wouldn't have gone through so quickly.'

'And has that made a difference?' Charlotte asked quietly.

'A huge difference! You've no idea how free I feel!' He glanced sideways, a rakish grin on his face. 'Well, maybe you have an inkling now.'

Charlotte smiled. 'You seemed like a man without a care in the world when we were on the beach.'

He squeezed her hand. 'I felt as if I'd been reborn.'

She swallowed hard but remained silent. Iannis's words affected her deeply. The intimate experience they'd shared had brought them closer together. She could feel the sensual tension that still existed between them. She hadn't wanted to fall in love with Iannis but that was what had happened. And there was nothing she could do to stem her feelings. To put it in medical terms, love was like a virus that struck you when you least expected it. And there was no known cure—at least not for the strong symptoms she was experiencing now!

The quiet period of emotional limbo she'd planned had been totally disrupted and she didn't know where this relationship was heading or indeed whether she could handle the new situation. It was one thing to make love on a deserted beach but something quite different when you put it in the context of the real world.

She guessed that Iannis, a newly divorced man, was feeling elated, uplifted by their love-making. But he wasn't ready for a meaningful relationship that would involve commitment. Neither was she…or was she? Her feelings were changing so quickly.

She ran a comb through her tousled hair, glancing in the passenger seat vanity mirror, as they approached the clinic.

Iannis parked in front of the building and turned off the engine.

'Would you like me to come inside and meet the mysterious stranger?' Charlotte asked as Iannis helped her down from the Jeep.

'Yes, please. I may need some help in...' His voice trailed away.

A petite, attractive woman with long dark hair and flawless olive skin was coming out through the front door of the clinic.

'Yassoo, Iannis!' The woman ran towards them, her strappy high-heeled sandals clicking noisily on the paving stones of the path, before standing on tiptoe to kiss Iannis's cheek.

Iannis's face remained impassive as he stared down at her. 'What are you doing here, Fiona?'

Fiona smiled, revealing small, impeccable, pearly white teeth in her pretty little mouth. 'I live here, remember?'

'Not any more you don't. You live in Athens with Lefteris.'

'I've come to see my parents and I thought you would be pleased to see me again. We could—'

'Fiona, I don't care what you thought. Our divorce is now final. You don't live on the island and you don't work at the clinic any more so—'

'Iannis, I don't want to upset you,' Fiona said in a wheedling tone. 'I'd like to talk to you, yes, so perhaps we could find somewhere quiet and—'

'I'll go inside the clinic and get on with some work, Iannis,' Charlotte interjected, feeling decidedly embarrassed by the whole scenario.

Running a hand quickly through her hair, she could feel grains of sand sticking to her scalp. Her clothes were crumpled and she knew she must look as if she'd been dragged through a hedge backwards. Although Iannis was now divorced, Charlotte experienced an irrational feeling of guilt, standing there in front of his ex-wife, having recently experienced the most wonderful love-making of her life.

Fiona turned to look at Charlotte. 'You must be the doctor who has taken my place.' Her brown eyes narrowed. 'My place at the clinic, I mean.'

Charlotte drew herself to her full height and held out her hand. It was a definite advantage to be tall but she wished she didn't feel quite so dishevelled in front of this well-groomed woman. The woman who Iannis must have loved when they'd first married. The woman who, from this recent display of affection towards Iannis, seemed still in love with him.

'I'm Charlotte Manners.'

'Fiona Kimolakis.'

The cool brown eyes were narrowing again. Charlotte noticed the dark eyebrow pencil outlining them, the soft muted eye shadow on the eyelids, the recently applied make-up on the flawless skin. Fiona's white cotton dress, cinched in at her tiny waist, made her look daintily pretty. In contrast, Charlotte felt as if she'd been caught stepping out of a hot, steamy bath without a towel.

'I'll come inside with you, Charlotte,' Iannis said evenly. 'We both have work to do. Fiona, give my regards to your parents when you get home. I'm sure Lefteris will be able to explain all the details of the papers that—'

'Iannis, darling, I'm not going home again until we've had a talk. These divorce papers I've received from your solicitor...'

Charlotte didn't wait to hear anything further as she hurried through the clinic door. The waiting area was deserted. Adriana was reading a book as she sat at the desk. She looked up when she heard Charlotte's footsteps.

Charlotte smiled. 'Everything seems quiet in here, Adriana.'

Adriana was a capable woman in her mid-forties who'd returned to nursing after bringing up her children. There was never any need to worry when she was in charge.

Adriana smiled back. 'Yes, we've had a quiet afternoon, Charlotte. Well, except for when Fiona lost her temper with Marina.'

'What happened?' Charlotte drew up a chair and sat down at the side of the desk.

'Fiona turned up, insisting that she wanted to see Iannis. Marina said he was out on a call and she didn't know when he would be back. Fiona started shouting, insisting that Marina give her Iannis's mobile number, which, of course, she wouldn't. Finally, Marina agreed to call Iannis. Fiona said she would wait here until he arrived.'

'Fiona met us outside when we arrived back from seeing Sophia,' Charlotte said. 'She seemed very calm when—'

'Oh, Fiona changes her mood by the second. Terrible to work with. She's a good doctor, I'll grant her that, but she can be a terror with the staff. We were all so pleased when she went off with Lefteris back to Athens.'

'Iannis must have been heartbroken when she left.'

Adriana gave a harsh laugh. 'Oh, Fiona had broken his heart a long time before that. Iannis was the one who sent her packing, insisted she go back to Athens with Lefteris. She didn't want to go. She'd never meant Iannis to find out that she was deceiving him. But I think Iannis had guessed what was happening and—' Adriana broke off, snapping shut the book she'd been reading and getting to her feet.

'I'll finish organising the treatment room, Charlotte,' Adriana said, loudly as Fiona and Iannis walked through the door.

'Do you think you could bring me a glass of cold mineral

water, Adriana?' Fiona said, smiling sweetly. 'I always used to keep some bottles in the fridge in Marina's office, so if you wouldn't mind…'

'Sorry, Fiona,' Adriana said. 'I'm simply too busy at the moment.'

She swept out of the waiting room, slamming the door of the treatment room behind her.

Fiona frowned. 'I've often found Adriana to be uncooperative, Iannis. I remember asking you ages ago if we could get rid of her and you said—'

'Fiona, as I keep reminding you, you don't work here any more,' Iannis said, in the patient voice that he usually reserved for truculent children. 'Charlotte and I need to get on with some work so why don't you go and stay with your mother for the night and then take the morning ferry back to Athens?'

'I'm not going back to Athens. Lefteris and I have split up.'

Iannis frowned as he stepped forward and put his hands on Fiona's shoulders. Watching the pair of them, Charlotte experienced a wave of something akin to jealousy.

Iannis and Fiona had been lovers, they had married, there was so much she didn't know about their relationship. Iannis might look annoyed now but he must feel something for the woman who'd been his wife. He had probably been furious when she'd cheated on him. But if he'd loved her deeply, he might have regretted the fact that he hadn't forgiven her and started again.

Charlotte turned away as she experienced the most awful feeling of *déjà vu*. It was happening to her again. She'd fallen for a married man. Well, Iannis was technically divorced now, but all the signs and symptoms she was witnessing seemed to indicate that this marriage was far from over.

'Go back to Athens, Fiona, and leave me alone,' Iannis said in an ominous tone. 'Our marriage is over. What you and Lefteris get up to is none of my concern.'

'But it should be your concern, Iannis,' said a shrill voice as a small, grey-haired woman hurried through the door. 'You can't turn Fiona away like this. It was your fault she left the island in the first place. Fiona was your wife. You should have taken care of her, not sent her away with Lefteris. She didn't want to leave, did you, my little one?'

The woman put an arm around her daughter's shoulders protectively.

Fiona pulled a tissue from her pretty little bag and dabbed her eyes. 'You were there that day, Mother, when I begged Iannis to let me stay, but—'

'That's enough!' Iannis's voice rang out around the surgery. 'Helena, please take Fiona home with you. We all know what happened and why I was forced to ask her to leave before. This is neither the time nor the place to start discussing—'

'Don't you speak to me like that, Iannis, you ungrateful boy,' the feisty Greek woman said indignantly. 'Where would you have been if I hadn't helped your grandmother to care for you after your mother died? Answer me that, Dr High and Mighty! You used to call me Mother when you were a little boy. Many's the time I did without food just to—'

'Helena, I am truly grateful for what you did for me when I was a child,' Iannis said, patiently and politely, clasping the older woman's tiny hand and looking down at her with kindly eyes. 'But that doesn't alter the fact that Fiona and I are now divorced and we must lead separate lives.'

Charlotte moved towards the treatment-room door, indicating to Iannis over the smaller women's heads that she was going to get on with some work. As she closed the door behind her she could still hear Iannis trying to pacify his ex-mother-in-law.

Charlotte leaned against the door, breathing heavily. Adriana smiled as she looked up from her task of removing sterile instruments from the steaming autoclave.

'The mother-in-law from hell,' Adriana said quietly. 'She was great as a second mother to Iannis when his own mother died, but she still thinks he's her little boy and he should do everything she wants him to do.'

Charlotte sank down onto the nearest chair as she heard the argument next door rising in another crescendo of accusations.

'So what really happened when Fiona went back to Athens?'

Adriana removed her sterile gloves and sat down next to Charlotte, leaning towards her in a conspiratorial fashion.

'Iannis must have known that Fiona had been carrying on with Lefteris behind his back. Lefteris was always coming over to Lirakis from Athens on the pretence of seeing Iannis. They'd been best friends at medical school. But there were rumours going round that it was Fiona he'd really come to see. I'm not sure what it was that brought it all to a head, but Iannis drove Fiona and Lefteris down to the harbour and waited until they were safely on the ferry.'

'He actually drove them to the ferry?' Charlotte queried.

'I think he wanted to make sure he was really getting rid of them. Fiona had led him such a dance during their marriage. There was also a rumour that Fiona was pregnant by Lefteris. Well, it must have been Lefteris because Iannis had moved out of the marital house and was living in the room he still has in the clinic annexe for the final months of their marriage.'

'So...' Charlotte hesitated. 'So it was rumoured Fiona was pregnant. Did she have a baby in Athens?'

'I heard she'd had a miscarriage, but again it's all speculation and—'

'Excuse me, a moment, Adriana...sounds like a patient has arrived next door.'

Adriana followed Charlotte, going back into the reception area of the surgery where the acrimonious argument was still raging. Iannis was totally ignoring the two women who'd once been part of his life as he tried to listen to an English tourist who was explaining that her son had suddenly become ill and she was desperately worried about him.

It seemed to Charlotte that the whole scenario was like the finale of one of those Greek tragedies where all the characters were talking at once just before somebody got stabbed! Firmly, she managed to persuade Helena and Fiona to come with her outside, away from the distraught mother and her son, who was now vomiting copiously into the bowl that Adriana was holding under his head.

'I think it would be better if you were to leave, ladies,' Charlotte said quietly. 'I'm sure Iannis will get in touch with you after he's dealt with his patient, but for the moment he'd got his hands full and—'

Fiona turned her pretty little face upwards to stare at Charlotte. 'Tell Iannis I shall be at my mother's house this evening and I shall expect him to call me.'

Charlotte took a deep breath. 'I'll pass on the message.'

She hurried back inside. The mother and her son were now in the treatment room with Iannis and Adriana. Iannis signalled to Charlotte to come and help him as he examined the boy.

'This is my colleague, Dr Manners,' he said to the mother. 'And your name is Mrs...?'

'Just call me Heather.'

'Well, Heather, if you would like to fill us in on the details of Andy's problems. You say he's recently vomited on several occasions. How long has this been going on exactly?'

'About six months, Doctor. It started round about the time his dad and I got divorced. I thought it was just that he was getting himself upset because he thinks the world of his dad and he couldn't understand how he could go off with that awful woman who...' The mother stopped and blew her nose. 'Sorry about that. It still hurts when I think about it.'

Charlotte put a hand on the mother's shoulder. 'Take your time, Heather. We're here to help you all we can.'

Adriana was removing the vomit bowl, plumping up a pillow so that Andy could sit up. He seemed to have recovered but Charlotte could see that the boy was far from well.

'Andy's just turned thirteen,' Heather said in a subdued voice. 'He's a good boy. He stays at home most evenings with me. He goes to his room, does his homework and he never gets into trouble, like some of the other boys at his school who are always staying out late. I know I can rely on my Andy. But lately he's been complaining of stomach cramps and he seems to have lost his appetite. Even though he doesn't eat much, he gets sick like he did today.'

Iannis was leaning over the boy. 'Hello, Andy, how are you feeling now?'

'I'm...I'm...a bit better, thank you, Doctor.'

Charlotte moved closer to the examination couch as she heard the slurred speech. She smiled at the boy as she placed her hand under his chin and lifted his face upwards towards her. There was a distinct rash around the boy's nose and mouth and his nose was running. She reached for a tissue and handed it to Andy so that he could wipe his upper lip.

'Do you ever get headaches, Andy?' Charlotte asked gently.

'I've got one now. They come on just before I'm sick. Look, I'm feeling better now, so can we go back to the chalet? I don't need a doctor. I told Mum I'd be OK if she just let me sleep it off...'

'Sleep what off?' Iannis asked evenly, as he looked across the couch towards Charlotte.

Charlotte gave Iannis a barely imperceptible nod of her head. They were obviously both thinking along the same lines. All the signs and symptoms were pointing to an obvious diagnosis.

Andy prevaricated, his fingers clutching nervously at the side of the couch.

'Well, er...well, like...sleep off feeling tired, wanting to be sick and all that,' the boy finished off, as quickly as he could get the words out.

He'd managed the end of the sentence without pausing, but his speech was still slurred. Charlotte held out her hands towards him.

'Let me help you up and then you can walk across the room. If you can reach the window without— Oops. Steady, Andy!'

Iannis caught their patient as he staggered forward, bumping into one of the trolleys and sending a couple of kidney dishes and a carton of gloves flying across the tiled floor.

'You're a little unsteady on your feet, aren't you, son?' Iannis said gently.

'Almost as if you're drunk,' Charlotte added quietly.

The boy sank back against the pillow. 'I don't drink alcohol! My dad used to drink something rotten. Mum used to get furious with him. That's why Dad's left her and gone off with that woman who drinks like a fish herself. I promised her I'd never drink like my dad did.'

'But you must be taking something to get you in this state,' Iannis said gently. 'I've got a very good idea of what it is, but I'd like you to tell me, Andy.'

Heather leapt to her feet. 'I don't know what you're implying, Doctor! My son is as good as gold. He's ill! That's why I've brought him to see you. If you can't do anything for him then—'

'Heather, have you ever noticed that Andy's mood changes from minute to minute?' Charlotte said quietly.

Andy's mother frowned. 'Well, yes, but he's at an awkward age, isn't he? That's all part of growing up. And what with his father leaving home and everything, I like to make allowances for him. And he's always suffering from sore throats, poor boy, and I have to keep him at home. Then he gets behind with his school work. So I thought I'd bring him out here for a holiday to perk us both up a bit. A bit of sun can work wonders, don't you think, Doctor?'

'I don't think sun will cure Andy,' Iannis said calmly, as he turned back to look at their patient. 'Andy, I want you to be quite truthful with me, otherwise I can't help you. Have you ever inhaled any solvents, such as glue, aerosol substances, cleaning fluids—'

'I don't have to listen to this!' Heather shouted indignantly. 'I didn't bring my boy here to be insulted! Come on, Andy, get off that couch, we're leaving.'

'It's OK, Mum,' Andy muttered.

Slowly and carefully he began to explain, pausing several times to get the words out.

'They're right. It's just a habit I've got into. I suppose I'm hooked now. Sometimes I can't get through the day without sniffing something. Doesn't matter what it is so long as it gives me a high.'

There was a look of horror on his mother's face as she sank back onto her chair and listened.

'The first time I sniffed something it was just for a laugh with the boys in the playground after school. I felt as if I was drunk and it was a nice feeling…till I was sick on the bus and the driver turned me off at the next stop. After that I used to buy an aerosol can or something like that on my way home from school and lock myself in my bedroom, pretending I was doing my homework.'

'But why, Andy?' his mother cried in an agonised voice. 'Why do you need to do this?'

'Because…because… I don't know any more, Mum. I felt a bit low when Dad left, I suppose. At first it was to get a high, now it's because I can't live without it.'

Charlotte put her arm on the mother's shoulder. 'Heather, you've got to accept the fact that Andy is now dependent on this habit, and he's going to need our help for a few weeks so that we can help him to kick it.'

'A few weeks! But we didn't plan to stay that long. I've got to go back to work. I don't earn very much but without it we couldn't manage. I've had to save every penny to get this two-week holiday and it was a cheap, last-minute cancellation. Can't you just tell Andy to stop doing it, Doctor, and—?'

'I'm afraid it's not as simple as that,' Iannis said. 'The dependency has taken a strong hold on Andy and it's like an illness. If Andy stays here on the island under supervision there's a strong chance we can cure him of the habit. But if you prefer to take him back to England and find a cure there, then—'

'No, no, I don't want the shame of it! His grandma would be furious with him.'

'There's no shame attached to this problem,' Charlotte interjected. 'A lot of adolescents experiment with substances. Most don't get hooked. Andy was unfortunate. But I think we've caught it in time. Now we must give him the treatment he needs.'

'You're being very kind about it,' Heather said, in a chocked voice. 'I only wish I could afford to—'

'Heather, if we could find you some work out here for a few weeks, would you consider staying on?' Iannis said.

'Absolutely!' Heather's expression brightened considerably. 'But what could I do? I'm a lunchtime waitress at the hotel near home.'

'You're a waitress at a hotel?' Iannis said. 'Perfect! One of my cousins has opened a new hotel in Lirakis town. He was telling me the other day that he needs more staff for the height of the summer season. Especially English staff who can talk to his guests in their own language. I'll give him a call this evening and make sure he pays you enough. He can afford it.'

'Would there be enough to pay the rent on the chalet we've taken for this two weeks?'

Iannis was looking doubtful now. 'Those chalets by the beach are for tourists so they're relatively expensive. There's an old cottage further inland going for a fraction of the rent you're paying now. Would you like me to speak to the owner? He's a friend of mine.'

Heather smiled. 'Oh, Doctor, would you?'

'I certainly would, Heather. Please, call me Iannis. Everybody does.'

'Thank you, Iannis,' Heather said shyly.

Watching and listening to this exchange, Charlotte could see that Heather was completely bowled over by Iannis's kindness.

'Are we going to stay on here, Mum?' Andy said.

'Would you like to, Andy?'

'Yeah! I really would. But I don't know if I'll be able to get by without sniffing just a little bit of something now and again. Not a lot, just a—'

Iannis put his hand on the boy's shoulder. 'Andy, from now on you've got to take your treatment seriously. What you're suffering from is like an illness. Charlotte and I can only cure you so long as you want to be cured. Do you want to be cured or not?'

Andy sat up, swinging his legs over the side of the examination couch. 'Yes. I want to be cured. Just tell me what to do.'

'That was a tense moment back there when you asked Andy if he wanted to be cured,' Charlotte said, swirling the ice cubes round in her glass of orange juice. 'I thought for a second or two that he was going to tell us he wanted to carry on as he'd been doing for the last few months.'

Iannis leaned forward and put his hand across the table to take hold of Charlotte's. They were sitting outside Stelios's taverna, the last rays of the sun falling across the water.

'That first step is so important. And often the patient says he wants to be cured and he doesn't mean it.'

Charlotte nodded. 'Solvent abusers can be very clever at covering their tracks. We'll have to keep the cleaning fluids locked away.'

'Adriana has already done that. As you know, I've called in Dora to special Andy tonight. She's a highly experienced nurse and knows exactly how to deal with this case. She'll continue with the treatment we've started and give us a detailed report in the morning. The first few days will be crucial.'

Iannis squeezed Charlotte's hand. 'It was a good thing

we were called back early from the beach this afternoon. Although I would have preferred not to have that awful confrontation with my ex-wife.'

He took a drink from his glass and leaned back against his chair. 'I thought I'd seen the last of Fiona when the divorce papers arrived last month, but it seems I was wrong.'

Charlotte put down her glass and gazed out across the fiery red and gold water. She took a deep breath, trying to calm herself by concentrating of the sheer beauty of the sunset. But tonight the sunset wasn't working its usual magic on her. She couldn't ignore the emotions churning inside her. She recognised that, yes, she was jealous of Iannis's ex-wife. Jealous of the proprietorial way she claimed Iannis's attention.

Fiona was an ex-wife and should know that she had no right to expect anything more from Iannis! Charlotte lowered her head, trying once more to calm herself. The other woman should have no hold on Iannis but it was nothing to do with Charlotte herself. It shouldn't be affecting her like this. Just because she'd fallen in love with Iannis out there on that sun-drenched beach…

'Are you OK?'

Charlotte raised her head and looked across the table at Iannis. 'I'm fine! A little tired. It's been a long day.'

'It was a wonderful day!' Iannis said. 'Apart from the Fiona incident.'

As Charlotte listened to Iannis's husky, sensual voice she found it brought back stirring reminders of their love-making. Yes, it was a pity that Fiona had turned up when she had to shatter the wonderful feeling of sensual elation that had pervaded every part of her body. Looking across at Iannis now, she could conjure it back if she tried.

But there was no disputing the fact that a dark shadow had fallen across their relationship with the arrival of Fiona.

'Do you think Fiona will go back to Athens tomorrow, as you suggested?'

Iannis gave a deep sigh. 'Not a hope! I tried to persuade her back there at the clinic, but then Helena joined in and tried to argue that it was my duty to care for Fiona.'

'But it's not your duty any longer! You're divorced.'

Iannis looked startled by Charlotte's vehement tone. 'Things aren't quite so simple now.'

Charlotte frowned. 'What do you mean?'

Iannis groaned. 'Don't ask! Look, let's order some food and then I'll explain the problem. I'm starving and I can't think straight when I'm hungry. We won't go into the kitchen. I'll just ask Stelios to bring us some grilled fish. The catch of the day. Would you like that?'

Charlotte tried to smile, but her mouth felt tense and tight. 'Sounds good to me.'

The *barbouni*, red mullet grilled on the barbecue outside the kitchen door, was delicious. As they ate, Charlotte was temporarily able to forget the image of that dainty, demanding ex-wife of Iannis's. Iannis topped up her glass with wine on several occasions and she didn't demur. Tonight she felt in need of something to blot out her conflicting emotions.

As she peeled one of the oranges that Stelios had put on the table at the end of their meal she looked across the table at Iannis. She didn't want to be the first to destroy the mellow ambience that existed but she knew she wouldn't be able to sleep until she'd found out why Fiona had such a hold on Iannis.

'That was a delicious meal,' she began with a smile. 'I didn't realise I was so hungry.'

'We did have an energetic lunchtime,' Iannis said, his smile rakish as he leaned forward. 'And, as I recall, you didn't eat very much.'

Charlotte could feel herself blushing. 'Didn't have time, did we?' She hesitated. 'So, what's this problem with Fiona?'

Iannis lowered his voice. 'Fiona's health isn't good. She shouldn't have left Athens. But now she's here...' He shrugged, as if to say that there was nothing he could do about it.

Charlotte frowned. 'What's wrong with her?'

Iannis glanced around him. 'I'll get the bill and we'll go back to my room. I don't want this to be spread over the Lirakis grapevine.'

Charlotte followed Iannis into his room. It wasn't far down the corridor from her own.

'It's amazing that I've never seen the inside of your room before.'

She sat down on the squashy sofa. Iannis joined her, stretching out his long legs in front of him.

He smiled. 'You won't believe how many times I've wanted to ask you in here, but I thought my intentions might be misconstrued. If I'd asked you in for coffee, you might have thought I was trying to seduce you.'

Charlotte smiled. 'I think I might. On the other hand, a cup of coffee wouldn't go amiss now. Just so I don't get the wrong idea, you understand.'

'Of course.' Iannis sprang to his feet and went towards the door of the tiny kitchen.

'It's just like my room along the corridor, only the other way round, if you know what I mean,' Charlotte said. 'Basic functional furniture. The door to the kitchenette is on that wall and I presume that other door over there leads to the bathroom. And you've put your bed in front of the window. Interesting arrangement.'

Iannis returned. 'I've switched on the cafetière. Let me tell you about Fiona while we wait.'

He leaned back against the sofa, placing one arm across the back. 'I had to end my marriage to Fiona because she was having an affair with Lefteris. That was why I moved in here. She begged me to go back to our house but I refused.'

'So you didn't think you could forgive her?'

'No chance! You see, Fiona and Lefteris had been lovers when we were all at medical school together. They quarrelled and Fiona turned her attention to me. I realise now it was simply to make Lefteris jealous, but I fell for it. Fiona and I had been friends since we were children. She's a year older than me, so when I was small I used to admire and look up to her. Fiona can be a very powerful woman when she chooses to exert her wiles.'

'I can imagine,' Charlotte said, ignoring the churning feeling in the pit of her stomach.

Why didn't she just get out of here now? There was no future in any kind of relationship where the man was involved in a relationship, even though the relationship was supposed to be finished. She should have learned her lesson by now.

'I think the coffee's ready,' she said quickly. 'I'll go and get it.'

She went into the kitchen and, leaning her hands against the sink, looked out over the moonlit garden of the clinic. She wondered why she had had the misfortune to fall in love with a man in such a complicated situation. Iannis was still grasped in the tentacles of that all-consuming, powerful woman. Fiona was small but she was as cunning as a viper.

Charlotte handed Iannis a cup of coffee a few minutes

later, and took a sip of her own. 'So, after you'd fallen for Fiona's plan to make Lefteris jealous, what happened then?'

'One thing led to another and we decided to get married. Far too quickly.'

'We have an English saying, ''Marry in haste, repent at leisure'',' Charlotte murmured.

'Exactly! Eventually we came back to Lirakis together to start the new clinic, and for quite sometime I thought we were happy. Then one of my cousins warned me that he believed Fiona was cheating on me but I wouldn't believe it at first. One day I found her in bed with Lefteris. I moved out immediately. All my love and respect for her died.'

'And now? The health problem you were telling me about?'

'Some months after I'd moved out, Fiona told me she was pregnant by Lefteris. She said she wanted me to go back to her and pretend the baby was mine. I laughed in her face, told her that was the last thing on earth I would ever do. I phoned Lefteris in Athens and told him to take care of his responsibilities. He came over to collect Fiona and unwillingly she went back to Athens with him. I even drove them to the ferry.'

So Adriana's account had been correct. That bit of the story had now been verified.

'And the baby?'

'Fiona miscarried when she was three months pregnant. Helena, her mother, told me this afternoon that the doctors had advised her not to get pregnant again for at least a year.'

Iannis paused. 'A few months later she was rushed into hospital with excrutiating pains and a high temperature. She was found to have an ectopic pregnancy. One Fallopian tube—the one with the foetus growing inside it—had to be excised. The other, according to Helena, is now completely blocked.'

'How awful for Fiona!'

For a few moments Charlotte was able to forget that this was the woman she had begun to dislike intensely, the woman who was causing her, for the first time in her life, to experience the most irrational jealousy.

'Fiona began crying this afternoon when her mother told me this. Apparently, Fiona is desperate to have a child, having been disappointed twice, but she's now afraid she will never conceive again. Helena is convinced that if the two of us got back together again in the house where we used to live, Fiona's health would recover. Of course, the whole idea of that ever happening—I mean, of the two of us ever being reconciled—is ludicrous and I told this to Helena, while Fiona simply dissolved into tears again.'

'What did Helena say?'

'My ex-mother-in-law has this way of speaking to me as she used to when I was young. When I was a child she used to discipline me, taking the place of my dead mother, overruling my grandmother, who was too old and tired to argue with her. I was always slightly in awe of Helena and I suppose I still automatically defer to her as I would to a parent.'

Charlotte experienced the most awful sinking feeling again. She put down her coffee cup. She couldn't take any more of this sob story. Yes, she was sorry for Fiona, but what Helena was trying to do was nothing short of emotional blackmail. Yes, she was standing up for her daughter but Charlotte didn't want to become involved in any more marital disputes.

'Iannis, I'm feeling very tired and I'm going to go back to my room now.'

Iannis stood up, looking down at her as he placed one finger under her chin to lift her face upwards towards his. Her mouth looked so inviting. So much had happened today. Making love to Charlotte after these weeks of longing for her had been more wonderful than he'd dared to hope. And then Fiona had arrived, casting her shadow once more over his life. Just when he thought he was going to be able to forget her completely and start a new, exciting, fulfilling relationship with Charlotte.

'Charlotte, do you have to go back to your room?' he said huskily, as he drew her into his arms. 'Today on the beach was wonderful, but tonight I'm longing to hold you in my arms again. No interruptions, just you and me together with the whole night ahead of us. Please, say you'd like to stay with me.'

Charlotte held her breath. The idea was so fabulously exciting. A whole night in Iannis's arms… But it didn't make sense any more. Not after what she'd just heard. A relationship with Iannis could turn out as disastrous as the one she'd experienced with James. Iannis was theoretically divorced, theoretically free, but all the complications he'd outlined would always be there in the background. He would never be free of Fiona and her family.

She stared up at him, her treacherous body trying to tempt her into a night of passion while her conscious, sensible mind was saying she should run from here and stay away.

'So, what's it to be, Charlotte?'

Iannis's words hung in the air. She looked up into his eyes and felt herself losing the battle. The tremors of sensual excitement running through her were too much to handle at the end of this long, emotionally draining day. As she found herself drowning in the liquid pools of his eyes she capitulated to her romantic self.

'I'll stay tonight,' she whispered. 'Just for tonight. Tomorrow…'

Iannis put a finger over her lips as he held her closer. 'No tomorrow,' he whispered. 'There's only tonight…'

Charlotte stretched herself under the crumpled cotton sheet. Beside her, Iannis was sleeping peacefully, one arm thrown above his head. Their love-making had been slow, unhurried, as if both of them sensed there really might not be a tomorrow and they wanted the experience of a lifetime to be encapsulated in one night.

Through the open window she could smell the scent of the roses in the clinic garden that managed to grow, despite the dry, unfertile soil, because every day the medical staff poured every scrap of water they could spare onto them.

Yes, this was a happy community. One of the best situations she'd ever lived in. She looked at the sleeping figure beside her. He seemed in his sleep as if he hadn't a care in the world. During the night he'd managed, temporarily, to convince her that he felt nothing for his ex-wife.

But was he deceiving himself and thereby giving her a sense of emotional security that could dissolve at any moment? She'd fallen hopelessly in love with Iannis on the beach. After their love-making during the night, she now loved him even more deeply.

But could she trust him implicitly? Wasn't she deluding herself, believing what she wanted to believe…as she had done with the treacherous James?

Quietly, she swung her feet to the ground and crept barefoot into the tiny bathroom in search of her clothes. Minutes later she was back in her own room.

Some time before dawn she fell into a deep sleep and dreamed that Iannis had gone back to Fiona. They were living in a beautiful house near the sea and when Charlotte walked past, Fiona came out onto the balcony and laughed at her, holding up the baby she was carrying in her arms.

'Iannis belongs to me!' Fiona was crying. 'You'll never have him. Go back to England where you belong. You don't belong here. This is my island, my Iannis, our baby!'

CHAPTER SIX

OUTSIDE the window in the clinic, some of the roses were wilting in the July heat.

'Adriana, has anyone watered the roses this morning?' Charlotte asked, as she began to clear up the treatment room after their last patient's examination.

Adriana lifted a bowl of washing-up water from the sink. 'The gardener was in early this morning and he gave them some water. I've just done the coffee-cups so they can have this water, too. It would be a shame to waste it.'

As Adriana went out through the side entrance to the garden, carrying her bowl, Charlotte went back to her desk to check the emails on her computer. It looked as if she might be free for the rest of the day unless there was a sudden emergency.

There was the sound of footsteps outside in the corridor. She looked up as Iannis walked in, wiping the sweat from his forehead with a large white handkerchief.

He grinned at her, his face more like a mischievous schoolboy's than that of an experienced doctor.

'Hope I wasn't missed too much this morning. I've been fishing with Stelios since the crack of dawn. We've got a good catch, so I hope you'll have dinner with me this evening at the taverna so we can sample some of it.'

Charlotte leaned back against her chair and smiled. She could feel her whole body relaxing again at the sight of him. For the last month, since they'd become lovers, she'd found herself recognising every little nuance of his character. And one thing she'd discovered was that he didn't like to be cooped up for too long. When he'd been working solidly for a few days he became restless. So when she'd got his message this morning on a scrap of paper pushed under her door, she hadn't been surprised.

The message had said, 'I need a break. My mobile's switched on if you need me, but give me a few hours if you can.'

She'd worried, as she always did, that he might have gone to see Fiona. His attention-seeking wife was still on the island and showed no sign of leaving. Everywhere Charlotte went she was reminded of Fiona's presence. If she and Iannis went to the taverna, sure enough, Fiona and her mother would turn up, expecting to be greeted in a friendly manner. Even though Iannis constantly tried to reassure her that he was merely being polite to his ex-wife and mother-in-law, Charlotte couldn't banish her doubts.

So hearing that Iannis had merely been out fishing was very reassuring.

'I wouldn't mind a break from work myself,' Charlotte said, as she switched off her computer.

'I would have taken you fishing if it hadn't been so early.'

Charlotte smiled. 'Oh, I don't mean early morning fishing. I'm glad you didn't wake me up. I'd prefer a break in the warm sunshine.'

'Come with me to see how Andy's getting on and then I'll take you out in my boat. Somewhere not too far round the coast. We're not busy today, and I can easily get back if there's a call from the clinic.'

Charlotte stood up. 'That's what I like about this clinic. The flexible working hours.'

Iannis smiled. 'Don't forget it works the other way. We're expected to go out in the middle of the night if there's a medical problem anywhere on the island. I'm glad you agreed to come with me a couple of nights ago to help deliver that baby.'

'All in the line of duty,' Charlotte said easily. 'How is the little mite we brought into the world?'

'Fighting fit. I called in yesterday afternoon and Maria and her baby girl are doing fine. Maria still hasn't chosen a name. I believe Teresa is favourite at the moment.'

'Teresa? That's nice.'

'Maria's grandmother was Italian, I believe. Maria's coming over to the clinic next week so you'll be able to see the baby again for yourself.'

'Good. I'll look forward to that.'

That was another thing that Charlotte enjoyed about working on Lirakis. The continuity of patient care. She became very involved with all the patients, those she'd met outside the clinic and those she'd treated when they'd come to the clinic.

'You know, Iannis, when I assisted you at that birth in the tiny cottage up on the hillside two nights ago, it was a completely new experience to me,' she said quietly.

'I've always been used to high-tech instruments and continuous monitoring, but up there we had to make do with our hands and the small amount of equipment we'd brought with us. We had to listen to the foetus with a Pinard's stethoscope and judge what was happening inside the uterus before deciding that we had to move things along. Good thing you'd taken some oxytocin with you.'

Iannis put his hands on Charlotte's shoulders, looking down at her fondly. 'You were a great help to me, especially after we'd safely delivered Teresa, or whatever she's going to be called, and Maria was too exhausted to cope with feeding her.'

Charlotte looked up at Iannis, basking in the warmth of his smile. 'Believe me, the most arduous task was boiling all that water on the stove. I'm used to instant hot water from a tap. Getting the baby to feed from the mother was easy. I'm glad we got there in time.'

'So am I. And I enjoyed having you with me afterwards when we celebrated the baby's birth.'

Charlotte could feel the hot flush on her cheeks as she remembered the champagne bottle that Iannis had produced from his fridge when he'd taken her back to his room. The celebration that had followed had not only been about the safe delivery of the baby. It had been a celebration of the love the two of them were now sharing.

She turned away as she felt her eyes moistening. How long could this continue? How long could she go on deluding herself that she had a future with Iannis when all the signs were that her fragile dream could vanish in a puff of smoke?

'Let's go and see Andy,' she said quickly. 'He was asking me earlier this morning if he could stay with his mum in the cottage full time now that he's supposedly cured.'

She fell into step with Iannis as they walked together down the corridor.

'Difficult question,' Iannis said evenly. 'How can we ever say a solvent-abuse patient is cured? It's one of those grey areas, isn't it? Certainly he's behaved well when he's spent the day with his mother at the cottage. And he's always come back here at night.'

'But there was that difficult episode when his mother was on the late shift at the hotel, wasn't there?'

Iannis nodded. 'That was the time I had to go and bring him back.'

Charlotte shivered as she remembered how worried she and Iannis had been. 'Andy had managed to get some glue and a plastic bag from somewhere, hadn't he? That could have been very dangerous.'

Iannis drew in his breath. 'It could have been fatal. Andy was actually trying to put his head in the plastic bag when I found him lying on the floor of the cottage. No, we definitely can't allow him to stay full time with his mother. Not yet. It's far too soon.'

Charlotte nodded. 'He's a good patient when it comes to taking his medication. That should be helping to reduce the craving by now. But there's no simple answer. If Andy gets depressed about something, he regresses. At the end of the day, only his own resolve will cure him. He's got to really want to be cured and we can't force that desire on him.'

'Andy seems to have very low self-esteem. I think he's met a few people in his life who've tried to belittle him,' Iannis said. 'We've got to try and show him that he's got a real contribution to make in this world.'

They went into Andy's room. The door was always left open, and there was a two-way mirror along one wall which acted as a window for the medical staff to observe Andy.

Andy was sitting in a chair beside the window that overlooked the garden. He was drawing on a sketch pad and was concentrating so hard that at first he didn't notice he wasn't alone.

'Hello, Andy,' Charlotte said. 'What are you drawing?'

Andy put down his pencil and turned round in his chair. 'Oh, I'm just doodling. It's not very good. I prefer painting actually, but I left my paints at home in England.'

Charlotte looked down at the intricate sketch of the garden that Andy had made.

'That's very good, Andy! I bet you get good marks at school in art class.'

Andy smiled. Charlotte couldn't remember having seen her patient smile before and she felt she was witnessing a breakthrough.

'Yes, I did get good marks, actually,' the boy said quietly. 'Not for little sketches like this, but the art teacher put one of my paintings on the wall.'

'What kind of painting do you like to do, Andy?' Iannis said.

'I like water-colours.'

Iannis smiled. 'That's fortunate. I've got a box of water-colours I bought as a present for one of my nephews. I found out he'd already got one exactly like it so I had to buy him something else. You're welcome to have them.'

'Wow!' Andy ran a hand through his hair, his eyes wide with excitement. 'You mean I could use them?'

'Oh, I'll give them to you. I've got no use for them. I don't mind painting my boat. I can make as many mistakes as I like—especially on the underside, which is mostly covered by water. The sea is very uncritical.'

Andy laughed. Charlotte felt a warm glow stealing over her. A smile and a laugh in such a short space of time. They were making real progress!

'Talking of which,' Iannis continued, 'the boat and the sea, that is. I've promised to take Charlotte out for a few hours, so we'll leave you to your sketching. I'll bring the box of water-colours over this evening.'

'Thanks very much. I hope you enjoy yourselves today.' Andy was looking wistfully out of the window. 'It's a lovely day out there.'

'Would you like to come with us, Andy?' Iannis said impulsively as he noticed the look of longing on the boy's face.

He had been looking forward to having Charlotte all to himself for a few hours but he couldn't bear to leave this poor child cooped up here all day. The treatment they were giving him consisted of much more than medication. Andy had started a fitness programme in the gymnasium. He swam regularly, under supervision, and he'd even attended one or two yoga classes before declaring it wasn't for him.

But Iannis decided there was nothing like a few hours of one-to-one therapy, or rather one-to-two, as Andy was going to be in the care of two doctors for the rest of the day.

The boy's eyes widened. 'You mean, come out in the boat with you? Ooh, yes, please!'

'Good, that's settled. You'll need swimming shorts and a towel, a jersey for if the wind blows up and…let me see…'

'I'll clear it with Andy's mom and get his things together if you go and finish off what you've got to do, Iannis.'

Iannis's boat was considerably bigger than Charlotte had expected.

'I'm amazed one person can handle a boat as big as this,' she said, as Iannis helped her on board.

Iannis grinned. 'Oh, it's much easier with a crew. Why do you think I invited you two along with me? You're both going to have to work your passage today. Andy, stay on the quayside for the moment. I've loosened the mooring rope. When I tell you to cast off, do you think you can undo the rope, throw it over to Charlotte and then jump aboard? You've got long legs and you look pretty agile to me.'

'No problem!' Andy said cheerily. 'I used to be long-jump champion at school before…well, when I was eleven. Haven't done much since, but I'm basically fit.'

'Great! I'll start the engine and then we can get moving.'

Sailing out of Lirakis harbour, Charlotte watched the receding harbourside, crowded with tourists and islanders. Looking up at the blue sky as she breathed in the salty sea air and the freshening offshore breeze, she decided that there was nowhere else on earth she would rather be. Especially now that she had two escorts for the day. Part of her had wanted to have Iannis all to herself, but she knew that this was a perfect chance to continue Andy's therapy. A chance that shouldn't be missed.

It had taken four weeks to gain the boy's confidence. Now they had to build on that. It was typical of Iannis that he should have suggested taking Andy out today. Iannis was generous to a fault. That was probably why he was so tolerant with his ex-wife and mother-in-law.

At least, she hoped it was simply Iannis's kind nature that came out when he greeted her two least favourite ladies with calmness and courtesy. She fixed her eyes studiously on the distant horizon as she made a strong effort not to worry any more about the women who seemed to have such a strong hold over Iannis. For today she would pretend they didn't exist.

'Hey, look at those big fish jumping around over there!'

Andy was excitedly pointing out over the edge of the boat.

'They're dolphins,' Iannis said.

'I've seen them on television but I never thought I'd get to see the real thing. Can I go and swim with them, Iannis?'

Iannis smiled. 'Not in this stretch of water, Andy. The current is treacherous on this part of the coast. You can swim when we get to the next bay, though whether the dolphins will follow us, I couldn't say.'

Andy hung over the side of the boat, trailing his fingers in the water, a broad smile on his face.

'A completely different boy to the one we've known,' Charlotte whispered, as she went over to Iannis who, with one hand loosely on the wheel, was keeping an eye on the dolphins.

'I think this is what he needs,' Iannis whispered back. 'A bit of family life.'

Charlotte hunkered down on her heels beside Iannis. 'We're hardly family, but I know what you mean.'

She sighed. 'I've always longed to be part of a real family.'

Iannis looked surprised. 'What do you mean? I know you haven't told me anything about your background but I've always imagined you led…how do you put it in English?…a sheltered life? Loving mother and father, sisters and brothers, grandmothers and…'

Charlotte smiled. 'Quite the reverse. Oh, yes, I've got a loving mother. The trouble was, she was never around when I was growing up. She's actually quite famous in one of the Australian soaps. I don't think she ever intended to have children. In fact, I know she didn't, but I was surprised when she actually told me. I was twelve at the time.'

Iannis put a hand over hers. 'You were twelve when your mother told you she never intended to have children? How did that make you feel?'

'Well, I'd always felt I was in the way,' Charlotte said slowly. 'I knew my mother loved me because she was always very demonstrative…when she was there, that is. But I used to get left alone in the flat in London with various so-called uncles or friends to look after me while Mum was out working. I'm not sure now what she did all the time, but she always managed to pay the rent on time. We were never turned out onto the streets.'

'I'd no idea! You look as if you come from this normal sort of background.'

'Years of practice.' Charlotte shrugged. 'I learned to fit in at school. Always got myself there on time even when my mum hadn't returned home. Washed and ironed myself a clean blouse or skirt the day when I needed to.'

She was breathing heavily. Whenever she remembered her early years nowadays she sometimes wondered how she'd survived. Her childhood had been so different to that of her friends, but she had simply accepted it.

'Kids always think it's the norm, don't they? If you love your parents…and I loved my mum, still do. Never knew my dad, but that didn't seem important when I was a child…you accept what life throws at you. I never went hungry. Especially after my mum got a minor part in a soap. She used to get back late at night after she'd been filming, wake me up because she'd bought a Chinese take-away on the way home and she thought I might not have eaten enough that day.'

'And were you happy to be woken up?'

'I was ecstatic! Oh, not for the food—I'd rather have slept on—but I craved my mum's attention. We used to giggle and laugh as we sat on the floor, eating straight from the boxes, licking our fingers over the spare ribs, watching some mindless late-night film on the television, Mum telling me how one day she was going to be a famous actress…'

'Your mum sounds a bit like my dad. Full of ambition but—'

'Oh, Mum's quite famous now in Australia,' Charlotte said quickly, feeling a surge of pride at the way her feisty mother had won through against all odds.

'She got her big break about ten years ago, which was around the time I was struggling my way through medical school. I was working in a pizza bar in the evenings and doing early morning office cleaning five days a week.'

'So you were completely independent by then?'

'Oh, I was independent from the age of fifteen. Mum answered this advert for English actresses to join a film company in Australia and off she went.'

'But didn't she want to take you with her?'

Charlotte felt the pain of separation once more. 'Yes, she did. But I knew it would disrupt my schooling. I'd spent a few weeks in hospital after I was knocked down by a hit-and-run driver. It made me want to work in the medical world. So, I'd set my heart on becoming a doctor and...well, I was doing quite well academically at the school I was attending in London. I was convinced I could pass the necessary exams and I wanted to stay focused. Anyway, Mum, although I love her to bits, is a very independent character. I would have only got in the way and been a drag on her career.'

'How often do you see your mother?'

Charlotte gave a whimsical smile. 'Hardly ever. I send her Christmas and birthday cards. She does the same for me...when she remembers. But I know she loves me and that's all that matters. I'm a big girl. I can take care of myself.'

Iannis gave a low whistle. 'You certainly can.'

'My mum is only seventeen years older than me. On the rare occasions we do meet up, it's more like being with an elder sister than a mother.'

Iannis turned back to the wheel as he guided the boat through a narrow channel between two groups of rocks. He was thinking how he'd known nothing about Charlotte's background. Her poise and confidence had convinced him that she came from a comfortable, well-heeled, English family. He'd even wondered if her parents had a medical background and she was carrying on the family tradition.

How wrong could you get? He could feel his heart going out to the poor little girl left on her own to cope with the problems of growing up. Perhaps this was why she was so strong, so focused when she dealt with the patients. Such a tremendous asset in the clinic.

He couldn't imagine life without Charlotte now. He couldn't imagine what it would be like when her contract ended and she was due to go back to England. He knew only one thing—that he had to persuade her to stay on. She might be battered and bruised from her disastrous relationship with that ex-boyfriend but he had to convince her that she could leave all that behind. Make her see that loving relationships really could survive.

It wouldn't be easy. She was like a fragile flower that would be crushed if he tried to rush things. He had to wait until he found she was ready for him, really ready. When he made love with her, he felt the warmth and love of her sincere personality. But he had no idea how she really felt about him. Yes, she responded, but he always felt she was holding something back. Always anxious not to give too much away.

Sometimes he caught her with a wistful, far-away expression on her face. Maybe she was already planning what she would do when she got back to London. He didn't know. He daren't ask. He had to wait until he was sure she would accept him without reservation.

'Wow! Look at that beach!' Andy cried out. 'There's nobody there. Why isn't it crowded with tourists?'

Charlotte laughed. 'Because we're miles from anywhere. You probably can't reach this beach unless you climb down those cliffs—am I right, Iannis?'

'You most certainly are, Charlotte. I attempted it once by land but it defeated me. You could probably do it if you brought rock-climbing ropes and all the other equipment experienced rock-climbers use. Some enthusiastic tourists do just that.'

He broke off and turned his head to look at Andy, who was still hanging over the side of the boat, dipping his hands in the sea.

'Andy, we're almost there. There's a particularly large rock we'll use to tie up the boat. It's over there. Can you see the one I mean? Are you ready?'

Andy was standing up, grinning all over his thirteen-year-old face. He'd never experienced an adventure like this. Nobody had ever taken him seriously before. He'd always just been the kid his parents wanted to get rid of so they could have one of their spectacular rows. But here he was with these two lovely doctors, being asked to do something really important.

'Andy, can you jump onto the shore from here?' Iannis said.

'Of course! Piece of cake!'

'Right! Go now. And, Charlotte, throw the rope to Andy. Andy, tie it round that big rock—OK?'

'Fine!' Andy smiled happily. 'Wow, this was fun!'

As soon as the boat was secure and he had changed into his swimming trunks, he ran along the soft white sand and went straight into the sea.

'Whee!' he cried, looking up at the blue sky, narrowing his eyes so he could gaze at the sun.

'Just look at that happy boy!' Charlotte said, as she helped Iannis to unload the boat. 'He's having a great time.'

'So am I.'

Iannis was staking out a flat section of sand and spreading towels over it.

'I'm so glad you invited Andy today,' Charlotte said, as she stripped to her bikini. 'It was just what he needed.'

Iannis drew her against him and looked down at her, a tender expression on his face. 'Was it what we wanted?'

'Let's just say it's different to what we'd planned,' Charlotte said gently. 'There will be other times when we can be alone.'

'Tonight perhaps?' he whispered softly.

She smiled, feeling the now familiar sensual arousal deep down inside her.

'Tonight,' she echoed. 'You promised to let me sample your catch of the day at Stelios's taverna.'

'I haven't forgotten. And afterwards? Will you—?'

Iannis broke off. Having caught sight of Andy striking out towards the deep water, he released Charlotte from his embrace and raced down to the shoreline.

'Don't go too far out, Andy. That's far enough. Swim back now.'

The boy turned and instantly obeyed, reaching the shore to find the two doctors standing in the shallows, ready to swim out to help him if necessary.

Charlotte put a towel round Andy's shoulders. 'Come and get dry. The sun's hot but the water's still cool.'

'Most Greeks refuse to swim in the sea until August,' Iannis said. 'Another couple of weeks before the swimming season is declared open.'

'That was great!' Andy said, throwing himself down onto the soft sand.

'Are you hungry?' Charlotte asked, as she started to unload the basket of food that the clinic cook had prepared for Iannis.

'I'm starving!'

At the end of their picnic, Charlotte tidied up the debris of chicken drumsticks, potato salad, green salad, tomatoes, and crumbs from the pastry of the spanakopita, spinach pies and the tiropita—delicious cheese pies—and lay back on the sand.

Andy picked up a small flat stone and skimmed it across the water. 'That hit five times! Did you see it, Iannis? Can you skim pebbles like that?'

Iannis searched for a suitably flat, round pebble and hurled it towards the sea.

'Wow! Seven times, Iannis!' Andy said. 'My turn again…'

Charlotte was vaguely aware of Andy and Iannis playing down by the sea but she found herself drifting off into a contented sleep. As she closed her eyes she promised herself that she would stay awake if she could. She didn't want to miss a minute of this precious day…

'Wake up, sleepyhead, it's time to go!' Iannis had his hand on her shoulder.

Charlotte stretched herself on the sandy towel. 'Did I fall asleep?'

'You've been asleep for ages!' Andy said, running up from the sea to stand dripping over her, shaking himself like a young puppy who'd just taken a bath.

Charlotte sat up and moved to one side to avoid the drips of water that were landing on her.

'And you haven't had a swim,' Iannis said, putting out his hand to haul Charlotte to her feet. 'Come on, this will wake you up.'

The three of them ran into the sea, splashing each other in the shallows before striking out at a quick pace away from the shore.

'Turn round now,' Iannis said, reaching out to touch Andy's arm. 'No further. I'm not in a lifesaving mood. You, too, Charlotte.'

She smiled. 'Ay ay, Captain!'

She swung round and began to swim back to shore. The three of them were spread out in line, Charlotte in the middle. She turned her head towards Iannis.

'Andy's an excellent swimmer for his age,' she said.

'Today has been a revelation of the boy's talents,' he

said quietly. 'The problem has been that he's been vastly underrated. It's up to us—'

'Look, that's a dolphin over there, isn't it?' Andy cried excitedly.

'Certainly is!' Iannis said.

The boy shot off in the direction of the dolphin that was cavorting in the middle of the bay.

'I'm going to swim with the dolphin. Dolphin, wait for me. I'm coming. My name's Andy and…'

Iannis quickly joined his patient and the two of them swam side by side. Charlotte swam back to shore and watched to see what would happen when they got near the delightful creature. It was as if they'd created their own marine life show out there in the bay.

'Oh, he's going away from us!' she heard Andy shouting.

'We've frightened him off,' Iannis said. 'Come on, Andy. We'll try again another day.'

'Promise?'

'Promise,' Iannis said solemnly, as he shepherded his young patient back to the sandy shoreline.

They loaded the boat and sailed out of the bay, hugging the coast as they turned back towards Lirakis town.

'I need to call in home to pick up the paintbox for Andy,' Iannis said as he steered the boat through the gap in the rocks.

'Where's home?' Charlotte said, intrigued by the idea that she might be going to see where Iannis lived when he wasn't in his clinic annexe room.

He'd sometimes referred to the place he called home but he'd never elaborated on where it was and she hadn't wanted to pry. As far as she knew, he seemed to regard his room in the annexe as his main base.

Iannis took one hand off the wheel and ran his fingers through his tousled hair, still damp from the sea.

'My home is a house by the sea in the last bay before we get to Lirakis town. My grandfather built it as an alternative to the family house in Lirakis town where my father was born. In those days you could only get over to the seaside house by walking on a rough track or riding on a donkey.'

'Is it still difficult to get there by land?' Charlotte asked.

'It's easy now. About ten years ago a road was carved out of the hillside and you can drive over there. But it was quite different when my father was a boy. I remember him telling me that during the summer holidays my grandparents used to load provisions on a couple of donkeys and they would go over to the house to live for a few weeks. It was cooler by the sea than in the town.'

'Did you live there as a child?' Andy had been listening in to the conversation.

'Sometimes we did. But mostly we lived in the town. My grandfather had died, my grandmother was getting old and my father went off to America. But I opened up the house after I was married and went to live there.'

Charlotte swallowed hard. So the house Iannis referred to as home was the place he'd shared with Fiona. She didn't like to think of Iannis living with her.

'Why don't you live there now, Iannis?' Andy asked.

'It's more convenient to live in the clinic annexe. I'm always on hand for my patients if they need me. Plus the fact that my wife and I are now divorced so I don't need a house.'

Iannis was turning the boat in towards the next bay.

'So there's no one there now?' Andy persisted. 'Can we go inside and have a look around?'

Iannis laughed. 'We'll have to because I'm not sure where I put that paintbox. You can help me find it, Andy.'

'That should be fun. Which house is it, Iannis?'

Andy had put a hand up to shield his eyes from the dipping rays of the sun and was scanning the shoreline.

Charlotte, looking across the water, could see several houses, widely spaced out close to the shore.

'It's that large one with the blue and white shutters. The balcony above the water has—' Iannis stopped in mid-sentence. For a moment the wheel seemed in danger of spinning out of control.

'There's somebody on the balcony, Iannis,' Andy said. 'It's a woman. Have you got a maid who does the cleaning or something?'

'No, I haven't,' Iannis said, his face grim as he grabbed the wheel again.

Charlotte experienced a tremor of dismay running through her as she watched the diminutive figure on the balcony. Even from this distance she could tell that the tiny woman in the red dress was Fiona. And the house…the house was exactly like the one in her dream. The house with the balcony where Fiona had taunted her by holding up the baby, laughing at her, telling her she would never have Iannis…

Charlotte turned away and sat down at the side of the boat, closing her eyes to blot out the sight of that odious woman. But with her eyes closed, all she could see were the remnants of the dream. How had she known what Iannis's house looked like? She'd never been here before but she vividly remembered the blue and white shutters, the wrought-iron rail on the balcony. Some people believed it was impossible to dream in colour, but she always did when it was something disturbing…

Maybe she'd simply thought she'd seen the house in a

dream. Perhaps she was transferring this present experience to that night when she'd woken up, drenched in sweat, sobbing in her sleep... Or maybe it had been a premonition. A warning. Something to remind her that her time on this island was limited. That she didn't belong here...that she should go back to England.

All that was needed now to complete the dream, or rather the nightmare, was for Fiona to be holding a baby in her arms. Wearily, Charlotte opened her eyes and stared across at the jetty in front of the house. Out of the corner of her eye she could see that Fiona was still standing on the balcony. But there was no baby, thank goodness! That much had been pure fantasy. Fantasy born of her own vivid imagination tinged with the most painful jealousy she'd ever experienced.

The baby had been a symbol of her subconscious desire for a family of her own. Loving Iannis as she did, she knew that her ultimate dream would be to have his child. So the nightmare she'd experienced, seeing Fiona with a baby, had signified that her rival had stolen that wish away from her...

'Are you OK, Charlotte?' Iannis asked, turning round from the wheel for a moment.

'I'm fine.' She stood up and joined him. 'Anything I can do?'

'You can help Andy to tie up, if you like.' He lowered his voice. 'We won't be staying long. Just long enough to find out what Fiona thinks she's doing in my house.'

'I'll wait here in the boat,' Charlotte said.

'No, no, I'd prefer you to come inside with me,' Iannis said quietly. 'I need you to help me look for the paintbox,' he added in a louder voice.

'Iannis, what a lovely surprise!' Fiona called, waving gaily from the balcony. 'Come in and have a glass of wine.'

'I'm not stopping, Fiona,' Iannis shouted in a steely voice, as he manoeuvred the boat against the wooden jetty. 'I came to pick something up and then I'm going straight back to the clinic.'

'Just one tiny little glass of ouzo, darling. You look exhausted. I'll go and get the bottle…'

Fiona turned away and disappeared inside the house.

With the boat firmly tied up, the three of them climbed the stone steps that led to the house.

The front door, also painted blue and white, was wide open.

'Come in! Come in, everybody! And who are you?' Fiona smiled up at the shy teenager.

'I'm Andy,' the boy said, gruffly, trying to get the words out without his voice changing back into its pre-adolescent mode.

'I'd no idea you were coming here today, Iannis,' Fiona prattled on, as she stood on tiptoe, trying to reach the side of his face with her lips.

Iannis took a step backward to deflect the kiss.

'Fiona, what the hell are you doing here?'

Charlotte took hold of Andy's arm. 'We'll go and look for that paintbox, shall we?'

Iannis flashed her a grateful look. 'It's somewhere in my study, Charlotte, second door on the left of the corridor leading to the sitting room. Try the cupboard next to the bookshelves.'

Charlotte escaped as quickly as she could, dragging Andy with her. She found the study and pulled the boy inside, closing the door and leaning against it to calm herself.

'Is that…is that Iannis's ex-wife?' Andy whispered.

Charlotte nodded. 'She usually lives in Athens but—'

'Iannis doesn't seem too pleased to see her, does he?'

'I think it was a shock, finding her here.'

The understatement of the year! Charlotte could hear the raised voices outside in the hall. Iannis was shouting in rapid Greek now. She couldn't follow what he was saying but his anger was blatantly obvious. Fiona was furiously screaming back at him then she changed tack and was pleading in her wheedling voice, interspersed with sobs.

'Let's look for that paintbox and then we can go back to the boat, Andy. I'm sorry you had to hear Iannis and Fiona arguing like this.'

Andy pulled a wry face. 'Oh, that's nothing compared to what my mum and dad were like when he got back from the pub, drunk. Dad used to beat Mum up when she started shouting at him. One night she was covered in bruises and one of her eyes was all closed up and I had to help her to go the doctor's in the morning.'

'Oh, dear, that must have been awful for your mother and also for you to be there in the house.'

Andy shrugged. 'Dunno. I got used to it, I suppose.'

'Let's look in this cupboard,' Charlotte said, pulling aside the stacks of paper and books. 'There! This looks like it.'

The paintbox was still wrapped in paper from the art shop in Athens where it had been bought.

'That's brilliant!' Andy said, clasping the box in his hands.

'Don't open it now,' Charlotte said quickly. 'We need to get back to the boat. We'll leave Iannis to continue his discussion with—'

The door opened. Iannis stood on the threshold, wiping a hand over his damp forehead. He was breathing heavily.

'Ah, you've found the paintbox. Let's go.'

'I haven't checked to see if—'

'It's all in there.' Iannis turned on his heel and began walking back towards the open door.

Charlotte had never seen him look so angry. She looked around her as they retraced their steps. There was no sign of Fiona and the house was completely quiet. Either Iannis and Fiona had settled their quarrel or agreed to differ.

Either way, it didn't alter the fact that Fiona's presence was always going to be a factor in Iannis's life. And Charlotte realised, sadly, that she mustn't get any further involved than she already was with Iannis.

What she'd witnessed had been a rehash of the painful situation she'd experienced with James. Iannis considered he was now a free man, but the unseen ties of his former marriage were still firmly in place.

And for the sake of her own self-preservation, she mustn't go down that road again…

CHAPTER SEVEN

STELIOS'S taverna was crowded this evening. Charlotte looked around her at the happy crowd. They were the usual people she'd come to know so well in the couple of months since she'd arrived here. Usually she went around with Iannis, greeting their friends and medical colleagues, some of them English, some Greek, before they settled at a table. Sometimes they would take a drink with Stelios at the bar before looking at the food in his kitchen.

But tonight, with the memory of his encounter with Fiona, Iannis wasn't in the mood for socialising. He'd promised Stelios he would bring Charlotte in to sample their early morning catch.

'There's a free table outside by the water,' Iannis said, putting his hand under Charlotte's elbow.

Charlotte felt relieved that they wouldn't have to pretend to be sociable this evening. They could sit quietly by themselves and, hopefully, discuss the events of the day. She didn't know whether Iannis would be any more forthcoming than he had been on the journey back across the water from his home.

They'd both made the effort to be pleasant when they'd taken Andy back to his room at the clinic. The boy had already unwrapped his paintbox and was excitedly starting his first picture when they left him. But the stilted conversation they'd engaged in when they'd walked down to the taverna had been atypical of their usual evening mood. Fiona's shadow lay across both of them.

'It's been a long day,' Charlotte said, as she sank down onto a seat at the water's edge.

The moon was already high in the sky, casting a luminescent sheen over the sea. Iannis poured out two glasses of wine from the bottle he'd picked up from the bar and drank deeply from his own.

'Yassoo!' He raised his glass and clinked it against Charlotte's.

'Yassoo, Iannis!'

Stelios arrived with a large platter containing three fish. 'Good evening, Charlotte, Iannis. Now, which of these special fish shall I grill for you this evening? This one here with the shiny scales perhaps? He was difficult to land, wasn't he, Iannis?'

Iannis gave a faint smile. 'Indeed he was, Stelios. He'll do fine, thank you.'

'Or you could have—'

'No, that one's perfect,' Iannis said, trying to disguise the fact that he was exhausted by the day's events.

'You know, Charlotte, two months ago, when my divorce came through, I thought all my troubles were over, but now I see they're only just beginning. That bitch of a woman—pardon my English…'

He grinned, and Charlotte felt relief at the first sign that Iannis's sense of humour was returning.

'That bitch has moved into my house and has no intention of leaving.'

'But didn't you say that was where you both lived when you were first married?' Charlotte said carefully. 'Perhaps Fiona regards it as her home as well.'

'I paid her off when she went back to Athens! My solicitor had a valuation done on the house and I paid Fiona half of it. My grandmother would have been furious if she'd still been alive. She never liked Fiona. When we were children she was always warning me against her. One time she called her a scheming little… Anyway, I didn't listen, did I? Otherwise I wouldn't be in this mess.'

'But how did Fiona get into the house? Surely you had the locks changed.'

Iannis gave a harsh laugh. 'Charlotte, here on Lirakis, we islanders rarely lock our doors. It just isn't necessary. Recently, during the summer when the place is swarming with tourists, some people have taken to locking their doors, but for the most part…' He spread his hands wide. 'It never occurred to me to change the locks. I didn't think Fiona would return except perhaps for a brief visit to see her mother.'

Charlotte swallowed one of the olives that a waiter had placed on their table. A dish of taramasalata had also appeared at the same time. She dunked a piece of pita bread in the pinkish cod roe paste and chewed thoughtfully.

'So, is Fiona planning to live there by herself? I would have thought she might be a bit lonely over in the next bay. Especially after the bright lights of Athens.'

Iannis took a deep breath. 'Fiona doesn't want to live by herself. But she somehow thinks that by taking possession of the house we used to live in, she can turn back the clock and persuade me to move back in with her.'

Charlotte stared at him, trying to ignore her furiously churning emotions. 'She can't be serious!'

'The thing is that Fiona, in her present precarious state of ill health, after a miscarriage and an ectopic pregnancy in the space of a few months, shouldn't be living alone and she knows it. She was even appealing to me as a fellow doctor, saying that she wanted me to live in the house with her so that if she needed medical help…'

'But that's emotional blackmail!'

Iannis nodded. 'That's what I told her. I said she had to

return to her mother's house or go back to Lefteris in Athens.'

'And do you think she will?'

'I've no idea. To be honest, I think her hormones are so disturbed after all her obstetric problems that she's becoming mentally unstable. She even threatened to commit suicide if I didn't return to take care of her.'

'Fiona needs medical attention...but not from you,' Charlotte said quietly.

'That's true. I wouldn't want to have her on my conscience.'

'But what about Lefteris? He's a doctor, isn't he? Where does he figure in all this?'

'I've tried to contact him in Athens. He's taken a three-month sabbatical, apparently. Nobody knows where he is. He took leave of absence soon after he and Fiona split up. I spoke to a friend who was at medical school with me and he's going to try and get a message to Lefteris. He thinks he may be travelling somewhere in Australia and he says he'll try out a few of his contacts over there.'

'Australia's a big country,' Charlotte murmured.

Iannis nodded. 'If the message does get through to Lefteris that I need to discuss Fiona's welfare, I should hear from him...that is, unless he's washed his hands of her. I wouldn't blame him if he had. She can try the patience of a saint. Yes, she's mentally and physically weak at the moment but—'

'Iannis, you can't take all the worry of Fiona on your shoulders. What about her mother? Can't she do something?'

Iannis sighed. 'Fiona has quarrelled with her mother. Surprise, surprise! They're not speaking to each other any more.'

Iannis took a deep breath. 'I've promised Fiona I'll call to see that she's OK when I can spare the time.'

Charlotte took a sip of wine as she thought over the implications of such a move. She was trying to remain impartial. As a doctor she could see that this kind of supervision was necessary but, on the other hand, the thought of Fiona exerting her considerable charms over Iannis…

'It's only a temporary measure until I can offload the responsibility onto Lefteris,' Iannis said. 'I'm sure I'll hear from him soon. We were the best of friends when we were medical students and I don't bear a grudge against him for breaking up my marriage.'

He gave a wry smile. 'With the benefit of hindsight, I ought to thank Lefteris for giving me my freedom from a life spent with the impossible Fiona.'

'That's one way of looking at it, I suppose.'

'Charlotte, you do understand, don't you?'

Iannis put his hand across the table to caress her fingers. She could feel her sensual self responding to his touch but she remained impassive. She'd already told herself that she wouldn't become any more involved. She would try desperately to keep her emotions under control. A light-hearted romance with Iannis was all she could hope for now.

The platter of grilled fish had arrived. Iannis began to slit down the backbone of the fish.

'It's a *lithrini*,' Iannis said, as he placed a succulent piece of white fillet on her plate.

'What's *lithrini* in English?' she asked, picking up her fork.

'I think it's sea bream.'

'Yes, this is sea bream. I recognise it now.' She swallowed the first mouthful. 'Mmm, it's delicious.'

They were both exceptionally polite during the course of the meal, both of them seemingly anxious to keep off the subject of Iannis's marital problems. But Charlotte could see the problem was weighing heavily on his shoulders.

When the fish had been cleared away and they were peeling their oranges, it was Iannis who resumed the subject.

'Fiona said the only way I could get her to leave the house was if she could move into the clinic annexe.'

Charlotte felt her spirits dipping again. 'And what did you say?'

'By that time I'd decided she was completely unhinged. I simply can't take her seriously any more. I told her the whole idea was ludicrous. That was when she stormed upstairs. There was a lot of banging of doors and then everything went quiet.'

'And we all went back to the clinic,' Charlotte said.

Despite her personal feelings, as a doctor she couldn't help herself from feeling worried about Fiona. When she put aside her dislike of the woman and viewed the case dispassionately, she could see that Fiona did need help, and if she was worrying like this, how much more must Iannis be worrying?

As if in answer to her unspoken question, Iannis said, 'I've phoned old Dr Pachos and asked him if he'll go over to see Fiona tomorrow. As I told you, he's retired but he said he'll get his son to drive him over during the morning.'

'Well, that's a relief.'

'Charlotte, you mustn't concern yourself with Fiona. She's my responsibility.'

'She's not your responsibility! When you divorced you absolved yourself from all that.'

Iannis looked alarmed. 'Charlotte, please, don't upset yourself. It's my problem, not yours. It really shouldn't affect you. When I can get in touch with Lefteris—'

Charlotte stood up. 'It does affect me, Iannis,' she said

firmly. 'I'm afraid I can't deal with your marital problems. I've been there before, remember? It's all too close to home for me.'

She could feel the tears pricking against the backs of her eyelids. The English couple at the next table were looking up at her, startled by her sudden change of mood. Charlotte realised she'd been keeping a tight hold on her emotions ever since she'd seen Fiona flaunting herself on the balcony, resurrecting that awful nightmare, bringing back all the pain and misery she'd suffered when she'd discovered that James wasn't to be trusted.

But her restraint had now vanished. She knew she was too tired to pretend any more. If she started to explain to Iannis how she felt she would completely lose control and make a complete spectacle of herself, here in the taverna. She had to get away, had to hide somewhere where she could lick her wounds far from the prying eyes around her now.

Wordlessly, she turned and hurried away, her feet clattering on the uneven cobbles of the waterside path. A cloud had obscured the moon and the black, velvety darkness was illuminated only by the tiny pinpricks of light from the small craft moored alongside the path.

'Charlotte, wait!'

Her heart thudded as she heard Iannis's voice. She continued to walk, increasing her pace. She had to be strong. She had to break off their relationship before it got any more serious. She couldn't cope with any more emotional pain. After James, she'd vowed she wouldn't get involved like that again. And yet here she was…

'Charlotte!' Iannis's arm slid around her waist.

She tried to pull away but he was drawing her against him, his fingers holding her tightly.

'I'm sorry to put you through all this,' he murmured

against her hair, his face nuzzling into her neck. 'Charlotte, you mean everything to me. You must realise that. I love you. And if I can dare to hope that you love me even half as much as I love you then I can see why you're so upset with the attention I'm giving to my ex-wife.'

Charlotte stayed very still as Iannis's arm encircling her waist made her feel utterly secure again. She was trying to put up some resistance but she was losing the battle.

'I love you, too,' she whispered, in spite of the warning voices in her head that were telling her Iannis had to be resisted. 'I don't want to get hurt again,' she said quietly. 'When I came out here I wasn't looking for a romantic involvement. I needed a period of calm to sort out my bruised feelings. And then you and I became lovers and you turned my life upside down. I don't know any more what it is that I want but—'

'I know what I want,' Iannis whispered huskily. 'I want us to be together, for ever. Will you marry me, Charlotte?'

She stared up at him. The cloud obscuring the moon had moved aside to allow some light to filter through onto the waterside path. She could see Iannis's expression now. His eyes held a deep tenderness that she'd never seen there before.

Her head was spinning. Never in her wildest dreams had she thought that Iannis would ask her to marry him. This couldn't be happening to her! If she could only suspend judgement. If she could only believe that she wouldn't get hurt again. James had asked her to marry him. James had placed a ring on her finger. She'd believed everything he'd told her but it had all been a pack of lies. James had had a wife in the background and…

'I can't marry you, Iannis,' she said carefully. 'Not until the problem of your ex-wife has been solved. I don't think you're ready to move on to another relationship yet and for the moment I need to be free of commitment. I can't risk making another mistake…all the agony that goes with splitting up and…'

Iannis placed his fingers against her cheeks, drawing her face upwards towards his lips, gazing down at her with such love and tenderness that she was almost ready to capitulate to any proposal that he might suggest. Almost ready…but not quite. Her strong sensible self was exerting itself. She was fully in control of her emotions again.

'OK, I won't ask you to make any long-term promises,' Iannis whispered, his warm breath fanning her face. 'But let's continue to be lovers without any commitment, if that's what you want. When you see how much you mean to me, I hope you'll reconsider my proposal. Until then…'

'No promises,' she whispered, as she felt her treacherous body reacting towards the man she loved so much. 'Let's live for the moment.'

As Iannis's lips came down on hers she knew she was lost again. But this time she'd set the parameters. She was going to try to remain as emotionally uninvolved as she could. She was going to enjoy her time with Iannis but she wasn't going to look into the future.

Iannis had asked her to marry him. But he hadn't thought through the implications. Hadn't realised that the ties of his former marriage hadn't yet been broken. Until they had, she wasn't going to gamble on her whole future.

Iannis opened the window of his room in the clinic annexe. The two of them leaned out over the window sill, breathing in the scented evening air which was still heavily laden with the perfume of the roses. Charlotte felt Iannis's arm tightening around her naked waist. She moved into the circle of his embrace, drawing him back onto the bed.

They'd already made love as soon as they'd got back to

his room—desperately, urgently, passionately. It had been a heady experience, each of them wanting to renew their pledge of love, to heal the rift that had threatened to tear them apart that evening.

The sheets had smelt as if they'd been freshly laundered that day. They were still crisp and cool, waiting to be wrapped around them during the long night hours when, satiated with their passion, they would eventually fall asleep in each other's arms as they had done so many times before.

Iannis reached up to close the window then he lay down beside Charlotte, taking her in his arms, his hands beginning to caress her slowly, tenderly, unhurriedly. They had the whole of the night to make love…

She could feel the fires of her excitement igniting inside her, the sensual electric current of her passion running through her as she gave herself once more to the heavenly ritual of their love-making.

'No tomorrow,' she whispered, as if to convince herself that this was to be the answer to all their problems.

She was drifting away from the earth on a cloud. Nothing mattered tonight except the consummation of their love…

For the next few weeks Charlotte managed most of the time to hold her emotions in check. She allowed herself to relax completely when she and Iannis made love, allowed herself to enjoy their off-duty time together, sailing in the boat, swimming in the sea, sometimes walking over the hills and finding a deserted beach where they could picnic, make love and then fall asleep in each other's arms.

Looking out of the clinic window now on this hot August morning, Charlotte felt that her policy of living for the moment was working. It was only sometimes, in the still dark hours of the night, on the occasions when she was alone in her own room, that she realised she was being totally unrealistic if she believed that she could give all this up and go back to England.

But what alternative had she? She didn't want to live in Fiona's shadow for the rest of her life. Lefteris hadn't got in contact with Iannis. Old Dr Pachos had tired of going over to see Fiona and Iannis had taken it upon himself to see Fiona several times a week. On the occasions when he went over to the house by the sea in the next bay, Charlotte found herself in an edgy mood. Until he returned she couldn't settle to do anything properly.

Fortunately, it didn't affect her work at the clinic. She could always concentrate on her patients without her thoughts straying to what might be happening to Iannis and Fiona, but when Iannis was away during her off-duty time, she experienced agonising jealousy until his return.

Fiona was still a very attractive woman. She might be highly strung and difficult but Iannis, having once loved Fiona, couldn't be entirely immune to his ex-wife's considerable charms.

'Sophia's here,' Iannis said, coming into Charlotte's consulting room. 'I've done a preliminary examination and now she's ready for her ultrasound.'

Charlotte stood up, took her stethoscope from the desk and put it around her neck. 'How is she?'

'Fine. She says the baby's kicking hard most of the time. Karlos is convinced it's a boy, wearing football boots.'

'It's good that Karlos and Sophia are in such good spirits, though I suspect some of it is putting on a brave front,' Charlotte said. 'They know that the blood serum screening indicated that it's unlikely their baby will be handicapped. But I'll be so relieved when the baby is born and any remaining doubts can be dismissed.'

Iannis drew in his breath. 'So will I. Meanwhile, we've

got to think positively. I now know that Karlos and Sophia are strong enough to cope with whatever happens.'

Charlotte fell into step with Iannis as they went down the corridor to the room where they performed their ultrasound scans.

Sophia was lying on the couch, her head already positioned on the pillow where she could watch the scan on the monitor screen. Adriana was preparing the gel to spread over Sophia's abdomen.

'*Yassoo*, Sophia,' Charlotte said. 'You're looking good.'

Sophia smiled. 'Good as in enormous, don't you mean, Charlotte?'

Karlos stood up to greet Charlotte. 'Sophia has a huge appetite now. Adriana has just weighed her and she's advised her to keep off the cakes and biscuits.'

'It's the baby who's got a sweet tooth, not me,' Sophia protested. 'Anyway, what time does the show start? Would somebody mind switching on the television? My little footballer is getting impatient to see himself on screen.'

Charlotte could tell that Sophia was putting on a brave face. She was understandably apprehensive, as they all were. Karlos also hadn't stopped his nervous chatter since he'd first arrived at the clinic.

'I must say I'm impressed by all this high-tech equipment,' Karlos said, sitting down on a chair beside his wife. 'Didn't think the clinic would be able to afford all this.'

'People are very generous when they know it's for a good cause. I put out an appeal in an international magazine when we first opened the clinic,' Iannis said. 'I was trying to tap some of the goodwill of our Greek expatriots. The ultrasound machine was donated about a year ago by a wealthy American family whose parents were born on Lirakis.'

'It must be a godsend for you, Iannis,' Karlos said.

'I don't know how we managed without it in the old days. The same thing with the X-ray machine. A group of Greek businessmen, now living in Australia, clubbed together and bought that.'

'Oh, look!' Sophia was pointing excitedly at the screen. 'There he is. There's Kyriakis.'

'Is that what you're going to call your baby if it's a boy?' Charlotte said, as she moved the scanner over Sophia's abdomen.

'We certainly are,' Karlos said. 'Kyriakis, after my Greek father who's still living in Australia. He'll be tickled pink when he hears.'

'Hold on, Karlos,' Sophia said. 'Wait till Iannis tells us what our baby is. We don't know for sure it's a boy. Just because he's kicking the living daylights out of me, it doesn't necessarily mean—'

'Hold it right there, Charlotte!' Iannis said. 'Look at that little appendage. Can you see it, Sophia? Right there at the top of that tiny leg…'

'Ha!' Karlos said triumphantly. 'I knew he was a boy. Well, I'll be blowed. Just wait until I tell my folks. My dad's dying for a grandson to take to football matches with him. Can somebody get a picture of our baby to send to my dad?'

Charlotte looked at Iannis. Everything now seemed normal with this pregnancy. She silently prayed that there wasn't any abnormality that the scan and the blood tests hadn't picked up. It was unlikely, given the blood serum screening and the images they'd seen on the screen. But, all the same, she would only be completely happy when the baby had been born and undergone a postnatal examination.

*   *   *

'OK, the show's over,' Charlotte said, switching off the monitor. 'Everybody enjoy it?'

Sophia was grinning happily as she clutched the photos of her baby which Iannis had just given her. 'Can't we have a second showing?'

Iannis smiled. 'Not for another month. Let me see. You're due in mid-October, aren't you? If you come to see us again in mid-September, that will probably be your last scan. I've made arrangements for you to have the baby here at the clinic. Charlotte has given you all the instructions about what you should do when you get the first signs that you're going into labour.'

'Make sure your bag is packed well in advance,' Charlotte said.

Karlos grinned. 'It's ready now. We've got everything ready except the baby. Sure you can't hurry things along, Doc?'

Charlotte smiled. 'Afraid not. Kyriakis will know when it's time to put in his first appearance.'

Adriana had left the room to take a call. She returned now to tell Charlotte she was needed in her consulting room.

'Another patient just arrived to see you. I think it's that English man who fell off the treadmill in the gymnasium.'

Charlotte glanced up at the clock on the wall. Richard Horton wasn't renowned for his sense of timing. Just when she was hoping to escape for some lunch!

She said goodbye to Sophia and Karlos, leaving Adriana to finish clearing up and arrange the next appointment.

As Charlotte walked back along the corridor with Iannis, he offered to see Richard in her place.

'I can probably deal with him quicker than you can,' he said with a wry smile. 'Richard would spend all day with you if he could.'

'I know, but I've got to be there for him,' Charlotte said quickly. 'He's depressed again. He'd like me to put him on antidepressants but I'm holding off for the moment. That's going to be my last resort.'

'What's the problem?' Iannis asked, slowing his pace as they approached Charlotte's door.

'Richard's wife has come out with the children. They've taken one of the holiday chalets over by the beach. Richard spends as much time as he can with his children, but his wife always makes a point of leaving him to it. He'd hoped this holiday reunion might turn into a reconciliation, that he could somehow win her over, but she's having none of it.'

'Is Richard's wife in another relationship, do you think?'

'Not as far as I know. She just doesn't appear to be interested in Richard any more. She's made the break and she's sticking to it.'

'Poor Richard. I know he can be a real pain, but I feel for him, unable to be with the woman he loves.'

'Yes.' Charlotte put her hand on the handle of her door. 'I'll see you later, Iannis.'

'I'm going to go and see how Andy's getting along. He's done so many paintings, I'm planning to put an exhibition on for him. The mayor says he'll put some of Andy's best paintings up for sale in the town square. The tourists will love those landscapes and seascapes of Lirakis that Andy's done.'

'He's making fantastic progress,' Charlotte said. 'We'll soon be able to discharge him completely. I'll be sad to see him go.'

'Me, too.' Iannis paused. 'When I've seen Andy I've got to go over to see Fiona.'

'Of course,' she said, with steely calm. 'How is she?'

'As difficult as ever, but her general health seems to be improving. She's more relaxed, not so tense as she was.'

Charlotte clenched her hands. 'Any news of Lefteris?' she asked.

Iannis shook his head. 'He's not back from his travels. I think the split with Fiona may be permanent and he's gone off to get her out of his system.'

Charlotte took a deep breath. It was all she good do to stop herself from screaming with frustration at the impossible situation.

'Can't blame him,' she said quietly.

'Absolutely not! We'll meet up this evening, then?'

'Why not?' she said lightly, as she turned away and went into her room.

As soon as she was involved in her patient's problems she was able to forget her own troubles. Richard began by pouring out his heart to her. His wife was totally ignoring him. She was going back to England with the children next week. He suspected she'd found another man. He couldn't take much more of this…

'Richard!' Charlotte reached across her desk and patted her patient's hand. 'You've got to let go. It's the only way you're going to be able to move on and find peace in your life.'

'Yes, but I've done everything Julia wanted me to do. I've stopped working all day and every day to earn a huge salary. I've sold the firm, started to live the simple life. Julia still has the family house, a good car, enough money in trust for the children's school fees…so what more can she want? Why can't she be happy with me like we were when we first met? I haven't changed all that much. I've lost loads of weight since I started my fitness regime and—'

'Richard, you must try to plan a new life without Julia. The children still love you. They'll always be there for you, but Julia is trying to exert her independence. I know it's hard but—'

'Hard! It's impossible! I don't think you've got any idea of what I'm going through, Charlotte.'

Richard banged his fist down on Charlotte's desk, causing the pens and pencils to rattle.

'Oh, but I have,' she said. 'I do know what you're going through, Richard. And I feel for you, I really do. But until you face up to reality...'

She heard her own words as if someone else had spoken them. Who was she to preach about facing up to reality? What was the reality of her hanging on here on Lirakis, hoping that Iannis would break the ties of his former marriage? That was never going to happen, was it? Not if Fiona had anything to do with it...and that small, determined woman was a force to be reckoned with.

She remained silent for a while, allowing Richard to rant and rave about the injustice of his situation. She felt at the moment that she could have joined in with his moaning, but she didn't say so. She simply made a vow to herself that she would face reality and leave Lirakis at the end of October. But how could she broach the subject with Iannis when he was still hoping she would stay on and wait for him to be completely free?

And wait...and wait...

No, she wasn't going to make that mistake again.

Charlotte walked back through the trees with Richard. He was a little calmer now. As they approached his chalet a couple of children came running to meet him, a boy of about twelve and a girl slightly younger. They seemed nice kids as they hugged their dad, each one taking a hand and pulling him towards the beach.

'Come on, Dad. You promised you would swim with us before lunch.'

Richard turned and waved to Charlotte as he disappeared in the trees at the edge of the shore.

'Thanks, Charlotte,' he called. 'You've been a great help.'

She didn't feel as if she'd really achieved anything. She'd simply listened to Richard moaning about his problems, which was all that anybody could do in a situation like this. It was up to each individual to make their own decisions about how they were going to solve their own problems and conduct their own lives.

She'd made her own decision and time was running out fast.

CHAPTER EIGHT

RICHARD HORTON had been into the clinic again that morning. He'd been more depressed than Charlotte had ever seen him and she'd finally prescribed antidepressants. It was a last resort but she felt that her patient needed a prop to see him through the next few weeks.

Since he'd poured out his heart to her last month, outlining his marital problems, she'd made a point of keeping an eye on him, ensuring that the health and fitness staff were aware of his volatile condition. She'd been heartened to hear that his wife had agreed to stay on until September with the children. But the extended holiday had only added to the poignancy of the approaching separation.

Richard's family were leaving next week, apparently, and the hoped-for reconciliation with his wife hadn't materialised.

Iannis opened the door and came in to perch himself on the edge of her desk.

'That was a long session you had with Richard this morning, wasn't it?'

'I had to give him extra time.'

'His wife still intent on leaving him?'

'Iannis, she already considers that they're separated. It's only Richard who's hanging onto his impossible dreams. And this particularly dream isn't going to come true. The sooner he can face up to that fact—'

'Life can be tough, can't it?'

She nodded. 'Even living here on this wonderful island,

people will always find a way of complicating their lives for themselves.'

'Is that what you think Richard is doing, Charlotte?' Iannis stood up and looked down at her, an enigmatic expression in his eyes. 'The poor man has no alternative. His wife refuses to take him back. Richard didn't make the complication. It was thrust upon him.'

'I know he didn't make the complication…not directly anyway. But he's got to accept that it's there. Just as…' She took a deep breath. 'Just as you've got to accept that Fiona is complicating your life. You can't move on until you've cut the ties.'

Iannis frowned. 'What ties? Fiona and I are divorced. I'm simply regarding her as a patient who needs my help.'

'Are you? Don't you think you're taking this all a bit too far?'

Iannis's eyes narrowed. 'I'd never thought of you as a jealous person, Charlotte, but—'

'All human beings suffer from jealousy if they find themselves in a position where someone is trying to steal the one they love.'

Charlotte clasped a hand over her mouth. There, she'd said it out loud! She'd voiced all the pent-up frustration of the past few weeks.

Iannis leaned forward and drew her into his arms. 'Darling Charlotte. Fiona means nothing to me. You've got to believe me.'

She flung back her head and stared at him. 'I want to believe it. I try to believe it. But it's impossible when that woman is still here on this island. I don't know what the two of you get up to when—'

'You've got to trust me, Charlotte. Without trust…'

'I've tried to trust you. I've suspended all my belief, but

it's no good. I've been hurt badly before. I can't risk ruining my life a second time.'

She pulled a tissue from the box on her desk and blew her nose vigorously before standing up and walking towards the door.

'Iannis, I've decided to go back to England when my contract expires next month. I think you should make arrangements with the agency to replace me.'

'No, Charlotte! Please, stay! You only have to be patient a little while longer and then—'

She turned at the door. 'My mind's made up, Iannis. Please, don't try to change it for me.'

She heard Iannis calling her name as she walked away down the corridor, but he didn't follow her. He'd finally got the message that she meant what she said. Returning to her room in the annexe, she felt a momentary sense of elation. She'd made a strong decision. This was all for the best. She couldn't spend any more time agonising over what would happen when she left Iannis.

She'd had the courage to take the matter into her own hands and she was now free. She lay down on her bed, willing the feeling of elation to remain, but it had already disappeared. In its place was a feeling of deep sadness tinged with despair. She still loved Iannis. Nothing would ever change that. Trying to stop loving him only gave her an empty void in her heart. There was nothing in the world that could replace that magic feeling of being in love.

It had been different when she'd split from James. That had been a slow, insidious realisation that James had not been all he'd seemed. Her love for him had died naturally. But this profound, intense feeling of love for Iannis which had consumed her now for so long wouldn't die a natural death. It would always be there.

She buried her head in the pillow to stifle her sobbing…

Minutes later, she sat up, went over to the shower room and washed her face. The decision had been taken and this was no time to start feeling sorry for herself. She had to bite the bullet and get on with her work for the next month. The patients mustn't suffer. By immersing herself in her medical work she would get through this crisis.

Adriana was sitting at Charlotte's desk, scribbling something on the message pad.

'Oh, good, you're back, Charlotte. Have you been to lunch?'

'Er, yes.' She would skip lunch now. Anyway she wasn't hungry.

Adriana stood up and came round the desk, holding out a piece of paper. 'Your phone was ringing so I took the call for you. Stelios, down at the taverna, wants to know if you'll see him some time today. He's worried about his chest.'

Charlotte pulled a wry face. 'I'm worried about Stelios's chest as well. I've been trying to persuade him to come and see me all summer. I'll call him back and get him to come in as soon as he can.'

'I've stopped smoking, Charlotte,' Stelios said, as he propped himself up against the pillow on the examination couch.

'When did you stop smoking, Stelios?'

'This morning, straight after breakfast—well, straight after the cigarette I always have with my coffee.'

Charlotte adjusted her stethoscope. 'Let me see, how many hours would that be?'

'Oh, it's quite a long time,' he said proudly. 'I feel terrible now and I'm dying for a cigarette but—'

'Talking of dying, Stelios, that's exactly what will happen to you, much sooner than it should, if you smoke another cigarette.'

He stared up at her with a startled expression. She realised this might have come as a shock to her friend but sometimes shock tactics was the best method of making an important point. She was only telling the truth. Wrapping it up in airy-fairy words wouldn't get the message across.

Looking at the thin ravaged chest that had rattled alarmingly when she'd listened in with her stethoscope, Charlotte felt a surge of alarm. She'd become very fond of Stelios since she'd arrived on the island. She didn't want to see him die prematurely.

Not that she would be here after October. She swallowed the lump that rose in her throat. Stay focused on your work, girl! Stelios has a lot more problems than you have!

'I thought I might just have the odd cigarette now and again—weddings and funerals, that sort of thing—because—'

'Your own funeral, perhaps?' she said quietly, placing a hand over his. 'You're not yet sixty, Stelios, and if you carry on like this, you won't make it.'

'You're really serious, aren't you, Charlotte?'

'Deadly serious. Now, slip this gown on and we'll go through to the X-ray room. I phoned for our radiographer and she should be there by now.'

As Charlotte studied the X-rays she could see several lesions. Silently she prayed that they might have caught it in time, but she was doubtful. The only time she'd seen an X-ray like this had been before embarking on a post-mortem examination in medical school. All the signs and symptoms of this case pointed to carcinoma. Years of smoking had irreparably damaged Stelios's bronchus and lungs.

'Adriana said I'd find you here, Charlotte,' Iannis said, as he walked in and went straight over to where Stelios was leaning back against his chair, breathing heavily.

'So you finally found enough courage to come and see Charlotte,' Iannis said in a bantering tone. 'I knew you wouldn't come and see me because you knew you wouldn't get any sympathy. All you've got to do is give up cigarettes and—'

'Iannis, will you come and look at these X-rays, please?' Charlotte interrupted briskly.

Iannis took the X-rays from Charlotte and held them up to the light in the window, then he took them over to the light-box on the wall and slotted the first one in place before switching on the light.

Carefully he looked through all the X-rays, taken from every angle, before switching off the light and pulling a chair near Stelios.

'You've got something of a problem, my friend,' Iannis said gently.

'I know that, Iannis. I'm going to die, aren't I?'

'We're all going to die,' Charlotte said evenly. 'But you're going to need some treatment to make you live a bit longer.'

'Treatment? What sort of treatment?'

Charlotte looked at Iannis questioningly. 'I know what I would recommend if I were in London,' she said. 'What's the usual procedure out here, Iannis?'

'We'll send Stelios to Athens for radiotherapy and chemotherapy. As soon as—'

'Hang on a minute!' Stelios said, in his alarmingly rattling voice. He paused for another coughing fit, raising his hand to show that he didn't want them to make any more plans until he'd had his say.

'I'm not going to Athens and that's final! I remember

when my elder brother Petros got what I've got— Oh, don't you two clever doctors look at me like that! I don't need X-rays and stethoscopes to make a diagnosis. I've got cancer, just like Petros had ten years ago. They sent him to Athens. He was there weeks and weeks and he still died. In hospital! Never came home again!'

'Stelios,' Charlotte said gently, sitting down on a chair on the other side of her friend. 'Treatments have improved in the last ten years. It would definitely prolong your life if—'

'I don't *want* my life prolonged. I've had a good life. Still enjoying myself. I'll take what's coming to me. But I'm not leaving Lirakis for any treatment, and that's final.'

'Iannis, I wish we could persuade Stelios to have some treatment,' Charlotte said.

They were sitting by the waterside early that evening. It had seemed only natural that they should go down to Stelios's taverna at the end of the day. Charlotte had hoped she could speak to her patient again but he was nowhere to be seen this evening. Probably keeping out of sight of the doctors who'd confirmed the diagnosis that he'd feared.

Iannis had made no mention of the fact that Charlotte was planning to work out her contract and then go back to England. The atmosphere between them was strained but they were keeping up appearances. Nobody watching them now would guess that their relationship was soon to be ended.

Charlotte knew that everyone considered them an item, expected that something would come of this whirlwind romance. She'd moved through the kitchen, choosing what she wanted for supper, her lips smiling so much that her cheeks ached with the effort.

Iannis leaned forward. 'Yes, I wish that we could persuade Stelios to go to hospital in Athens. But he's a stubborn old boy. I remember when his brother died he told me that if ever he got the same illness he wouldn't bother with all that hospital treatment. He'd just stay here until his time was up.'

Charlotte drew in her breath. 'One way round it would be to give him his chemotherapy here on the island and then afterwards he could be admitted to hospital.'

Iannis touched her hand with his own. It was the first contact today and she felt an involuntary shiver running down her spine. She held her breath until the sensation had died down.

'Charlotte, we have to respect his wishes and leave him to make the biggest decision of his life. This isn't London. This is Lirakis. We do things differently out here. He has a loving family who will support him in whatever he decides to do. Family is everything here on Lirakis.'

She knew that was true. Even ex-family seemed to be important to Iannis. She banished the pang of bitterness that swept over her. She couldn't change Iannis any more than she could banish Fiona from the island.

She looked down at the food on her plate. Usually she enjoyed stuffed aubergine but tonight she had no appetite, which was strange considering she'd had no lunch.

A distraught woman was running along the darkening footpath close to the water's edge. 'Help! Help me! My husband swam out to sea ages ago! I can't see him any more. I think he's drowning. Can anybody here help me?'

Iannis and Charlotte were already on their feet. Charlotte had already recognised the woman as Julia, Richard Horton's wife. She moved forward to meet her.

'Julia, take us to where you last saw Richard.'

'It's round here, on the edge of the beach. You can see where he's put his clothes. The children were watching television in the chalet. I happened to be at the other end of the beach and I saw him swimming out, just swimming towards…'

Julia had run out of breath as the three of them hurried round to the beach. Behind them a crowd was gathering.

In the darkening twilight it was impossible to see the horizon. A pinkish glow still hung over the sea, illuminating it in parts. But there was no sign of Richard.

Iannis was already stripped to the waist. 'I'll see if I can find him.'

'Iannis, be careful!' Charlotte cried as she watched him sprinting down the beach.

If anything happened to Iannis she knew she would never get over it. She would never get over splitting up with him, but at least she would know he was alive. And going back to England next month, sooner rather than later, would ease the pain of separation. The longer they were together here on Lirakis, the harder it would be to recover.

Disjointed, irrational thoughts were running through her mind as she waited on the shore, clenching and unclenching her tense hands.

Please, come back soon, Iannis! she silently prayed. Don't take any chances.

The light had completely faded now. The crowd on the beach was getting restless.

'Was that the doctor who swam out just now? Where's the lifeguard, then?' somebody said.

'They don't have a lifeguard. It's only a little island, remember? Everybody has to muck in here and look after each other. I pity that poor doctor. I don't fancy his chances out there in the dark. Do you think he's…?'

Charlotte moved away so that she wouldn't become any more worried than she already was. Straining her eyes out to sea, she was sure she'd seen a ripple on the surface of the water…beyond the outline of the rocks. Yes, somebody was swimming back to shore…

'Iannis! Iannis!' she screamed, wading into the sea, oblivious of the wet cotton dress clinging to her legs.

The shadowy form was getting nearer. Yes, she could see him now. And, miracle of miracles, he was holding a body against his chest, swimming backwards, kicking hard with his legs to propel himself and the inert form towards the shore.

Charlotte was up to her waist now. She knew she mustn't go any further. Her professional training was coming to the fore again. If there was any life left in Richard she would have to help save him. And for that she needed to keep calm and not waste her energy.

She reached out towards Iannis and together they hauled Richard onto the shore.

'Stand back, everybody!' Charlotte said loudly. 'Please, give us some room here. That's right… More space, please…'

She was down on her knees, the wet sand clinging to her clothes as she felt for Richard's pulse. Not a flicker. He looked grey, lifeless, as if there was no hope of him ever being resuscitated.

But they had to try! Never give up until the patient was pronounced dead.

She turned Richard on his side and a frothy liquid gushed out of his mouth. She cleared his airway. Now to perform CPR.

'We'll work in tandem,' Iannis said, as he tried to recover his own breath.

Bringing the heel of his hand down hard onto Richard's breastbone, he pressed rhythmically a couple of times before leaning back on his heels.

Charlotte took a deep breath, pinched her patient's nose and began mouth-to-mouth resuscitation.

Iannis checked again for a pulse and shook his head before recommencing cardiac massage.

Charlotte's turn again to try mouth-to-mouth resuscitation. The cold body beneath her seemed completely lifeless. She was aware that Julia was standing close by, watching every movement, her eyes moist with tears. Charlotte found herself spurred on. She had to get a response from Richard. She had to save him! Maybe if she saved him…

'Charlotte, I can feel a pulse!' Iannis cried.

She sat back on her heels, a wave of exhaustion sweeping over her. She could see a slight movement from Richard's chest.

'He's breathing! Richard's breathing!' Iannis said.

Charlotte smiled with relief as she saw her patient's mouth opening. Richard made a gurgling sound and then his eyes flickered open.

'You didn't have to save me,' he muttered groggily. 'I wanted to die. I still want to…'

'Richard! Oh, my darling Richard!'

Julia, in her beautifully cut designer dress, was kneeling on the sand, her arms around her husband. 'I thought we'd lost you! I would never have forgiven myself if anything had happened to you.'

Richard closed his eyes. 'Julia. I didn't know… I thought you…'

'Hush, my darling, the doctors need to get you back to the clinic and then we'll talk.'

'Don't leave me, Julia.'

'I'm coming with you in the doctor's car. Don't worry, I won't leave you.'

Adriana had arrived, driving Iannis's Jeep. Between them

they managed to get Richard onto the back seat, his wife sitting in the front between Charlotte and Iannis.

'You're still there, aren't you, Julia?' Richard called faintly from the back seat.

Julia turned round and patted Richard's hand. 'Yes, I'm still here, darling. I'm not going anywhere.'

'Do you think what Richard did was a cry for help, Iannis?' Charlotte said, as they drank a celebratory glass of wine at Stelios's taverna much later that evening.

'That's difficult to say,' Iannis said carefully. 'Richard had swum a long way out and lost all his strength. He couldn't have got himself back. He'd actually sunk beneath the surface. It was only the buoyancy of the sea that brought him up again, otherwise I wouldn't have been able to find him. He was, to all intents and purposes, a drowned man.'

Charlotte shivered. 'I'm glad you were able to save him. Julia seems anxious to make up for lost time and be reconciled with her husband. It's strange how a crisis like that can change everything. It's certainly had the desired effect for Richard.'

'I only hope this reconciliation will last,' Iannis said quietly. 'When the euphoria evaporates, will they resurrect their old differences?'

'Who knows?' Charlotte said. 'Love does strange things to people, doesn't it?'

'It certainly does.'

Iannis was watching her now, a strange, enigmatic expression on his face. She'd been so worried about him this evening. But she mustn't make any changes to her plans. Although her love had deepened…if that were possible…nothing had changed their situation here on Lirakis.

She was still the outsider in Iannis's family and she had to leave him to get on with his life.

As if reading her thoughts, Iannis said, 'I phoned the agency in London this afternoon and asked them to review the list of candidates for your post as from the end of October.'

She swallowed hard. So Iannis had finally accepted it. She hadn't expected him to be so quick in responding.

'It's not so important for me to have another doctor in the winter usually but the Greek tourist board plans a succession of out-of-season activities here—painting courses, a music festival, that sort of thing—so extra medical help will be needed.'

Iannis was holding his hands behind his back, his fingers crossed as he told the necessary lie. The latter part of his information was true. The tourist board was planning to attract tourists over the winter. But he had absolutely no intention of contacting the agency.

If his strategy worked, if he feigned indifference to Charlotte's departure, maybe she would change her mind. He knew of no other way to get through to her. Pleading would be of no use. She was a determined character and only if she considered that the decision was hers and hers alone would she change her mind.

He smiled across the table, feeling a surge of hope as he saw the blatant dismay on Charlotte's face. Yes! She hadn't expected him to accept that she was leaving Lirakis. Maybe his plan was working already. He hoped so because he hadn't got any more tricks up his sleeve. He would just have to wait and see what happened and pretend he didn't care.

Well, Richard Horton's plan had worked. Maybe it had been a cry for help. Maybe he'd hoped that Julia would come to her senses if she thought he was going to die. Richard had taken a dangerous gamble.

Now it was his own turn to raise the stakes. After all, he'd got nothing to lose. His own life wouldn't be worth living if he couldn't spend it with Charlotte.

'I'm going back to the clinic,' Iannis said evenly. 'Are you coming?'

Charlotte looked across the table in surprise. Iannis had always assumed that they were going back together. But tonight was different. Tonight they were no longer an item. Tonight she would go back to her own room and lie awake…

Depressing thought! But she couldn't backtrack now. Not when Iannis had accepted her decision.

She stood up. 'Yes, I'm coming now.'

They walked along side by side, hands almost touching but not quite. Back at the clinic, Iannis said he would look in on Richard, make sure he was OK.

'Shall I come with you?' Charlotte asked.

Iannis shook his head. 'No need for both of us to be there. I'm only keeping him in the clinic for the night. We can discharge him in the morning. No, you go and get some sleep, Charlotte.'

He bent his head and brushed her cheek with his lips. She held herself in check, wanting the contact to last longer, her treacherous body reacting to his touch. But he was already turning away, walking along to see his patient and the reconciled wife who was keeping watch in the chair at her husband's bedside.

Charlotte felt a pang of doubt as she watched Iannis walk away. She was doing the right thing, wasn't she? This was all for the best. Making a clean break was the only way.

Sleep was impossible that night. She tossed and turned, reviewing the events of the day, puzzling over Iannis's new attitude to her. He'd accepted her imminent departure. He was already moving on.

She would have to do the same. After all, that was what she wanted, wasn't it?

CHAPTER NINE

For the next week, Charlotte made sure she was fully occupied every minute of every day. She didn't want to think about the future. Very soon she would have to contact the hospital in London, let her old boss know she wanted to resume her career where she'd left off. But not yet. It was only the middle of September. She was trying to convince herself she had plenty of time.

It was easy during the day to keep busy. There was a constant flow of patients at the clinic requiring her attention. There were more people on the island now than in August. Many tourists seemed to be taking late holidays this year so she didn't have time to think until the evenings.

Iannis hadn't asked her to join him for supper this week. She had no idea where he was spending his evenings but it wasn't with her! Fine! He was getting used to the idea that they'd split up. He'd accepted it much better than she had. Whenever she met him in the clinic, he seemed perfectly happy and at ease with the situation.

She tried to feel glad but her perverse nature still craved the idyllic life they'd shared together during the summer. She was only human, she couldn't fall out of love immediately, even though she was trying to harden herself.

This evening, at the end of a long hot day when she hadn't had a moment to herself, she would have liked to have sauntered down to the taverna for some supper. She knew she could join one of the groups of people she knew on the island, but that wasn't what she really wanted so she'd opted for a sandwich and an early night. She leaned back against her pillows, munching on the sandwich the clinic cook had given her. Salami and tomato. Not her favourite, but it would stop her feeling hungry during the night.

Was she feeling sorry for herself? No, she definitely wasn't! She was coping admirably. Sticking by her decision, ready to move on…

She sighed as she reread the same sentence again. None of this story she was reading was sinking in. Perhaps it was just a lousy story. It shouldn't be. She usually enjoyed this author. Her other books had been—

'Charlotte!'

She jumped, dropping the sandwich onto her book. Iannis was hammering on her door.

'Can I come in?'

'Yes, the door's unlocked.'

Iannis burst in. 'Karlos has just phoned me. He thinks Sophia's gone into labour.'

'Oh, no! She's not due for another month.'

'I know. I've asked him to bring her in, but Sophia's too scared to travel in the state she's in. We'll have to go out there. I mean, you will come with me, won't you?'

'Of course! I'm not surprised that Sophia is scared. If anything happens to that precious baby… Oh, dear, I can imagine how nervous she must be feeling!'

Charlotte swallowed hard. The thought that she and Iannis were finally going to deliver this much-wanted baby was terrifying. But even more scary was the fact that they weren't one hundred per cent sure the baby would be totally normal. She told herself, as she always did, to think positively, otherwise she would be no use to the patient. Concentrate on the practicalities.

She was already out of bed, rushing over towards the

shower room, carrying jeans and a T-shirt in one hand and dropping the unfinished sandwich in the bin with the other.

'Give me two minutes to get dressed and I'll be with you.'

She was vaguely aware that Iannis had caught a glimpse of her awful nightdress, the one she'd torn soon after she'd come out to Lirakis and had never got around to mending. She'd been wearing this unattractive, crumpled garment for at least three nights. She wondered fleetingly if Iannis was comparing her frumpy appearance with the carefully groomed, leg-waxed, lotioned and perfumed woman who'd shared his bed more times than she cared to remember.

The road over the hill to Sophia's cottage was completely dark. The streetlights didn't extend this far. In the beam of the headlights Charlotte saw a goat running ahead of them with a small kid beside her. Both animals were terrified by the bright lights of the Jeep.

Iannis slowed down, driving at walking pace until the animals made for the edge of the road and disappeared from sight down the valley. He revved the engine and took the next bend at a faster pace than Charlotte felt was safe. She gripped the side of her seat.

'Sorry, Charlotte!' Iannis took one hand off the wheel to reach across and touch her arm. 'I didn't mean to frighten you.'

'I'm OK. I understand the need to get there as quickly as possible, but let's get there all in one piece, shall we?'

The touch of his hand on her arm had unnerved her more than the screeching of the tyres round the hairpin bend. She was edgy again. Trying to hold onto her emotions when she was close to Iannis was sheer agony.

Iannis brought the Jeep to a halt at the end of the path

beside the sea. Charlotte tried to keep pace with him as he hurried ahead of her towards the lights of the cottage.

Karlos came outside the cottage as he heard their voices. 'Thank goodness you're here. Sophia's in terrible pain. I just don't know what to do. I've boiled some water. You always need water, don't you? I saw it on a film once when—'

Karlos was prattling along, his nerves getting the better of him.

'Karlos, shut up,' Sophia said, raising her head off the pillow. 'Just sit here beside the bed and let me hold your hand. Oh…oh, it's coming again. Iannis, Iannis, what do I do? I think—'

'Pant, Sophia,' Charlotte said. 'Pant like this, you remember how I showed you. You mustn't push yet.'

In the brief examination Charlotte had been able to see that Sophia's cervix was fully dilated. The waters had broken. The head was visible at the entrance to the birth canal.

She wiped the sweat off Sophia's forehead as she watched Iannis carefully easing the baby's head out. Next came the shoulders and then, in a slurry of blood and mucus, the rest of the baby was born.

They'd only just arrived in time. Sophia had been in an absolute panic when they'd arrived. She could well have pushed at the wrong moment and caused harm to herself and the baby.

'It's a boy!' Karlos said. 'I knew it was. Kyriakis. Oh, he's so tiny.'

'You might think he's tiny,' Sophia retorted, 'but he felt as big as an elephant just now. Is he all right, Iannis?'

Iannis was cutting the cord. She pulled a dressing sheet from her bag and wrapped it round the baby.

Kyriakis was now crying lustily, his tiny red face all puckered and angry-looking.

'I don't think he meant to come out so soon,' Karlos quipped, as he admired his son. 'It was probably a whole lot cosier inside Sophia's tummy than in the outside world. Shall I go and get a feeding bottle or something? Perhaps he's hungry.'

'I can feed him myself,' Sophia said, putting the squalling infant to her breast. 'The bottles I bought are purely for emergency use only.'

Iannis looked over the heads of mother and son and smiled at Charlotte. She smiled back, trying without success to swallow the lump in her throat.

What on earth was she doing, turning her back on a life out here on this island? How could she simply walk away and pretend it meant nothing to her? How could she resume her life in England when she'd lived here with Iannis all through the heady days of summer?

'We're going to take you back to the clinic, Sophia,' Iannis said. 'We'll make you comfortable on the back seat with the baby and Karlos can sit in the front with Charlotte and me. We need to do some postnatal checks on you and the baby and it will be much easier back at the clinic.'

As the Jeep bumped its way back over the hill towards the clinic, Charlotte was sitting in the middle of the front seat, her arm pressed against Iannis. She felt every slight movement of his body as he changed gear, turned the wheel, moved in his seat. And she couldn't get rid of the feeling that she was moving inexorably towards a most unsatisfactory end to her time here on Lirakis.

Looking up at Iannis's face, his set, determined expression, she felt she didn't know him any more. He'd been acting strangely all this week when she'd met him in the clinic. He'd so obviously been avoiding her. It was as if he couldn't wait for her to finish her contract.

'How about a nightcap?'

Charlotte looked up at Iannis, surprised at his suggestion. They were walking along the corridor back to the annexe, having settled Sophia, Karlos and the baby in one of their larger rooms.

Charlotte had wondered if this four-week premature baby would need to be put in an incubator. But his little lungs were breathing adequately so they'd decided he could sleep in a cot beside his mother. The night nurse was on hand and would contact Iannis if there was a problem.

Iannis paused outside his room and looked down at Charlotte enquiringly.

She hesitated. 'Yes, I'd like that,' she said.

She was feeling so vulnerable, so weak-willed all of a sudden. All she wanted to really do was throw herself into Iannis's arms and beg him to forget everything she'd said about leaving the island.

'There's something infinitely moving about watching a couple having their first baby, isn't there?' she said softly as she curled up on Iannis's sofa, tucking her legs underneath her. 'I've noticed it before when I've delivered a firstborn infant. The parents are so wrapped up in each other. It's wonderful to watch.'

Iannis sank down onto the sofa, holding out the bottle towards her and pouring some champagne into her glass.

'I was saving this bottle for a special occasion and I decided this was it,' Iannis murmured.

'You mean wetting the baby's head, don't you?'

'Of course. What else is there to celebrate?' He raised one eyebrow.

She took a sip. Iannis was watching her. She sensed that

he wasn't taking her seriously. Almost immediately her head felt light. She was losing all her resolve. Well, she hadn't been close to Iannis for…how long? At least a week. And it was having a disastrous effect on her.

Iannis leaned across and took her glass from her hand, placing it firmly down on the table at the side of the sofa.

'I think you've had enough of that,' he said, his lips twitching.

'I hope you're not suggesting that I'm drunk.'

'You haven't had the chance. I was thinking how beautiful you look when you relax and take that look off your face.'

'What are you talking about?'

'I'm talking about the miserable expression you've worn all week.'

'Well, I've had nothing to smile about,' she said heatedly. 'And if you're simply going to insult me, I'd like my glass back and then I really will get drunk…so that I can forget…so that I'll stop thinking about… Oh, Iannis…'

He was folding her into his arms, holding her so close that she thought she would never breathe again. She felt crushed in more ways than one. All her resolve had gone. Whatever the outcome, this was where she belonged. Here in Iannis's arms…

He was lifting her up, carrying her over to the bed, whispering in her ear, telling her he loved her desperately.

'Stop fighting me, Charlotte,' he groaned. 'I can't live without you. I've tried but it's impossible. Please, please…'

'Yes, oh, yes,' she whispered as he held her against him, his hands discarding her clothes, stroking her skin, caressing every part of her until she moaned ecstatically and capitulated completely.

* * *

She lay back amid the rumpled sheets and looked up at Iannis. As she'd wakened and opened her eyes, she'd found him gazing down at her with an intensely tender expression.

'I gambled everything in the hope that you'd come back to me,' he whispered. 'You are here to stay, aren't you?'

She nodded. For the moment nothing else mattered but her love for Iannis. Later she would come down to earth and try to make sense of her life.

'It's been the longest week of my life,' she murmured.

'Me, too.'

'But, Iannis, you looked so happy, so together whenever I saw you.'

'Then I'm a better actor than I thought I was. Hold on, I'd better answer the phone. It might be the night nurse about Sophia.'

She watched Iannis's expression turn to one of amazement. 'Lefteris! Where the hell are you? I've been trying to get in touch with you for weeks. Oh, Marcus told you, did he? So you've already spoken to Fiona. So what...? Ah, I see...'

Iannis was smiling now. He reached across and squeezed Charlotte's hand.

'Well, that's great news. Glad you two have made it up... Yes, I wish you all the best... No hard feelings at all. I'm very happy for you. I've got some good news for you myself...I'm hoping to get married again. Yes, I've proposed once but you know what women are like. She's holding out on me but I think I can wear her down if I persist...'

Iannis put the phone down and turned to look at Charlotte.

She smiled. 'So you're going to try and wear me down, are you?'

He grinned. 'One way or another. First, I'm going to confess that I didn't contact the agency.'

'But you said—'

'I know. A little necessary white lie. I took a gamble and it seems to have worked. You've come back to me, but you haven't answered my all-important question.'

Iannis climbed out of bed and knelt beside her. 'Charlotte, will you marry me?'

She paused just long enough to make it look as if she was considering other options before she leaned over the side of the bed and agreed that, yes, it was the only thing in the world that she really wanted and she hadn't been able to sleep all week for thinking about what she'd turned down.

Moving out from the tiny church on the hill above Lirakis town into the bright October sunlight, Charlotte felt as if she was still in a state of shock. She had no idea how Iannis had managed to organise the paperwork and appease the priests who had been concerned about his divorce and considered at first that six weeks wasn't long enough to prepare his English bride for their approaching nuptials.

A generous donation to the church funds had helped to change their minds and Charlotte had been utterly committed to finding out all she could about the Greek way of life. Or rather the Lirakian way of life, because it seemed to her that the traditional way of holding a wedding on Lirakis was an art form in itself.

She smiled now as Iannis drew her against him to oblige the photographers with a wedding kiss that would appear in the Lirakis newspaper.

'Are you OK?' he whispered, as they drew apart.

'Never better,' she whispered back. 'And I didn't put a foot wrong, did I? I must admit I didn't understand half of what the priests were saying but I responded in the right places, didn't I?'

Iannis's eyes glowed with pride as he looked down at her. 'You were magnificent. Everybody loved you—especially me. And you look fabulous in that white gown. If only my grandmother could see you!'

Charlotte smiled as she glanced down at the ivory satin wedding gown that had been totally restored for her. The surviving, much-younger sister of Iannis's grandmother had preserved it for decades, wrapped in tissue paper inside the cold cupboard built into the hillside at the back of her house. As soon as Iannis had told her about the impending wedding, Great-Aunt Anna had produced the garment.

Iannis had been doubtful if it would survive the ceremony, but as soon as Charlotte had seen it she had known this was the dress she wanted to wear. She had tried it on and it had fitted perfectly. And so a whole army of relatives had begun the task of replacing the lace, sewing on endless covered buttons down the back and letting down the generous hem, because Grandmother Kimolakis had been considerably shorter than Charlotte.

'Do you think your grandmother would have approved?' Charlotte whispered.

'Of course she would.' Iannis leaned forward and kissed her on the lips. 'That kiss wasn't for the cameras.'

She felt a shiver of delicious anticipation. Tonight, when everyone had gone home…

'Hey, Iannis!' one of the photographers called out. 'Do you think you could postpone the honeymoon till later and turn and face the camera again?'

Iannis smiled obligingly as he tucked Charlotte's arm through his.

Charlotte looked around her at the smiling faces. It seemed as if the whole of Lirakis had turned out to watch the wedding. Medical colleagues, friends, tourists still lingering on in the Indian summer, patients… She caught sight of Stelios sitting on a bench under one of the trees, lighting up a cigarette.

Ah, well, she wouldn't nag him any more. Now he'd explained he was at peace with himself she would simply have a chat with him when she could escape from the well-wishers crowding round her. Make sure he really was OK…whatever that meant in his case. She'd spelt it all out to him, but she knew that you could lead a horse to water, but you couldn't make him drink.

Not when he was a stubborn old horse like Stelios.

He was still sitting under the tree when Charlotte managed to escape a little later. Defiantly, he puffed on his cigarette, trying to check the cough that rumbled in his throat.

'Charlotte, if you've come to—'

'I haven't,' she said gently. 'I've accepted what you told me. I respect your decision.'

'You do?' Stelios said gruffly. 'Well, in that case, I'll come to your reception and raise a glass to the pair of you. I wish you every happiness and lots of children. Children are the biggest blessing in life you can have. Mine are standing by me now. They know the score as well as I do and I know they'll be there for me…at the end.'

'I'm sure they will,' Charlotte said, spreading out her fragile skirts so that she could sit down on the bench beside him.

He put a hand on her arm. 'Keep him happy, Charlotte. I remember Iannis when he was a little boy. Always smiling, always happy, even though his mother died and his dad left him. He deserves happiness now.'

'I'll make sure I make Iannis happy. And who knows? I might give him his first child sooner than anybody expects.'

She winked at Stelios. 'Keep that under your hat.'

For a second the older man looked puzzled. 'My hat?'

'Keep it to yourself. I just thought you'd like to know. Only found out myself this morning.'

Stelios grinned. 'I can keep a secret. Congratulations!'

Charlotte hugged the secret to herself. What a perfect ending to her wedding day that would be when she told Iannis.

Stelios stubbed out his half-smoked cigarette as he started coughing again.

Charlotte waited until he'd finished. No preaching, she told herself sternly. It was too late for that.

'You know, Charlotte,' he said, 'I've always been a rebel.'

'Surprise, surprise!'

He grinned boyishly. 'I'm not going to put myself through it like my brother Petros did. Endless treatments, X-rays, medication. Pah! I'm enjoying myself now. Doing what I want. Sitting in the sun. Fishing when I feel up to it. My children have taken over the taverna. I'm taking my medicine—'

He leaned forward conspiratorially. 'It's a special linctus my grandmother used to make. Does wonders for my cough, especially if I mix it with brandy. And when the end comes…'

He shrugged his shoulders and spread his hands wide. 'When the end is in sight, you and Iannis will be around for me, won't you, Charlotte?'

Charlotte swallowed hard. 'We'll be there Stelios.'

'And that morphine you gave me once when I had a bad coughing fit? That seems to help.'

Charlotte gave him a wry smile. 'Anything else you'd like to self-prescribe while I'm here?'

He grinned. 'You're a good doctor, I'll give you that. We may not see eye to eye about treatment but I wouldn't change you for anything.'

* * *

She went inside the marquee that had been erected on the field next to the church. Iannis waved across at her, his eyes beseeching her to help him out. It appeared that Richard and Julia had just presented him with a large cheque to be used as they felt necessary at the clinic.

'That's extremely generous of you, Richard,' Iannis was saying when Charlotte managed to ease her way through the crowded marquee.

'Not at all,' Richard said. 'You literally saved my life.'

Their patient turned and looked at Charlotte. 'And our beautiful bride kept me sane when I thought I was going mad.'

'I must add my thanks, too,' Julia said, holding onto her husband's arm. 'We've both decided to compromise. Richard has decided that the simple life isn't for him so he's arranged to go into partnership with an old colleague. They'll share the responsibilities equally. They're both family men who've realised that the most important thing in their lives is the family. They should earn enough for a comfortable lifestyle but they're going to change their priorities.'

Richard squeezed his wife's arm. 'Julia has been so supportive since we got back together again.'

Julia smiled. 'I'm not going to be so…so demanding in my standards. I'm going to accept that Richard needs to work and if—'

'I'm never going to work the long hours I did before.' Richard turned to look at the bride and groom. 'We're going back to England tomorrow. We only stayed on for your wedding. As you know, we sent our children home to stay with my parents so they could go back to school for the autumn term. We'll be back next year, all four of us, for a proper holiday.'

As Charlotte watched Richard and Julia going crossing the floor of the marquee she felt relief flooding through her. Richard had been a difficult case and she could never have dreamed way back in May that things could have turned out so well for him.

Richard and Julia had stopped to chat to Sophia and Karlos. Sophia was showing off their baby and the older couple were admiring the tiny infant, who was now thriving. After his shaky start, little Kyriakis was fighting fit and living up to his expectations—according to his parents—of being a budding footballer.

'Charlotte, you look stunning!'

She turned at the sound of the young voice. 'Andy, I'm so glad you could come.'

'And Mum's here, too. The hotel caterers wanted her to waitress for them but she said, ''Oh, no, today I'm a proper guest''!'

'I should think so, too,' Iannis said.

'We're off back to England next week. I'll have loads of work to catch up at school.'

'I bet you'll be top of the art class,' Charlotte said.

'I've sold lots of paintings in the town square! The mayor's invited me to come back next year. He's going to pay for Mum and me to come out and stay in a chalet at the town council's expense. Apparently, I'm a tourist attraction.'

Iannis smiled. 'I hope you'll find time to come out in the boat with us next year, Andy. We still haven't swum with the dolphins.'

'Yeah, that'd be great!'

'I never thought we'd be alone again!' Iannis said to Charlotte as they relaxed in their bedroom overlooking the sea.

Charlotte had managed to persuade Iannis that, since Fiona and Lefteris had gone back to Athens, it was a crying shame not to take over the Kimolakis ancestral home. She'd convinced him that she didn't want to sell it and buy somewhere completely new. All the ghosts of his former marriage had been banished when his ex-wife and her lover had left the island.

Charlotte had enjoyed renovating the place. It was a lovely house and there had been no shortage of relatives and friends willing to help her change the curtains, polish the wooden floors, buy new carpets and rugs. A helpful gardener was now employed and the shrubs and flowers he'd planted complemented the old trees that had been there in Iannis's grandfather's day.

'I think most people wanted to come back to the house and continue the celebrations all night,' Iannis said. 'We'll have a big party here on our first wedding anniversary, but for tonight…our wedding night…I want to have you all to myself.'

'I've got something to tell you,' she whispered, snuggling against him. 'You know that day when I accepted your proposal and you threw all your condoms in the bin…'

Iannis was staring at her, wide-eyed. 'But that was only six weeks ago. You can't be—'

'I haven't had a period since then so this morning I took a test.'

'Darling!' He clasped her in his arms. 'Are you…are you really…?'

'Yes, I'm really going to have our baby. So there'll be one more person at our first wedding anniversary. Possibly two. My mum phoned to say she was too busy to make it to the wedding but she'd try to get here for our first wedding anniversary. I can't imagine her as a grandma!'

Iannis smiled. 'We may have more than one baby. There are several sets of twins in my family.'

He kissed her tenderly on the mouth, his desire for her mounting as he held her closely against him.

'Whatever! The more the merrier,' she whispered, as she felt a shiver of delicious anticipation running through her.

A whole night together, the rest of their lifetime here on Lirakis. And after the baby was born she would stand on the balcony holding it up so that everyone could admire it.

Her dream would finally have come true…